Lindy froze su ... **you say?' she ju** ... **to croak.**

'I've just told you that I won you in a poker game last night,' he informed her indifferently, turning and strolling to the door. He paused as he reached it. 'By the way, when your husband turns up—tell him he's fired. I did mention it to him last night, but he was probably too worse the wear for drink to remember... I dare say the fact that his wife is now mine to enjoy has also slipped his memory, so perhaps you'd be good enough to remind him of that too. And, by the way—I've had your things moved into my suite.'

Dear Reader

As spring leads into summer, many people's thoughts turn to holidays. This is an ideal time to look out for our holiday reading pack featuring four exciting stories—all set in the beautiful British countryside. The Yorkshire moors, Scotland, the Isle of Wight and Cornwall will be the glorious backgrounds to these four wonderfully romantic tales. Let us know what you think of them, and of stories set in the UK in general. Would you like more of them, or do you prefer more exotic climates? Do tell.

The Editor

Kate Proctor is part Irish and part Welsh, though she spent most of her childhood in England and several years of her adult life in Central Africa. Now divorced, she lives just outside London with her two cats, Florence and Minnie (presented to her by her two daughters who live fairly close by).

Having given up her career as a teacher on her return to England, Kate now devotes most of her time to writing. Her hobbies include crossword puzzles, bridge and, at the moment, learning Spanish.

Recent titles by the same author:

CONTRACT TO LOVE
TWO-TIMING LOVE

NO MISTRESS BUT LOVE

BY

KATE PROCTOR

MILLS & BOON LIMITED
ETON HOUSE   18-24 PARADISE ROAD
RICHMOND   SURREY   TW9 1SR

*First published in Great Britain 1992
by Mills & Boon Limited*

© Kate Proctor 1992

*Australian copyright 1992
Philippine copyright 1992
This edition 1992*

ISBN 0 263 77606 9

*Set in Times Roman 10 on 11¼ pt.
01-9207-55360 C*

Made and printed in Great Britain

CHAPTER ONE

THE very first time Lindy Hall had seen Niko Leandros her breathing mechanism had all but seized up on her; and on subsequent meetings, despite decided reservations as to his character, she had found her fingers itching to reach out and ascertain for themselves whether or not that vision of male perfection comprised actual flesh and blood.

'Where is your husband?'

And that was another thing about him, reflected Lindy, lack of sleep dulling her normally alert mind—his voice: its unmistakably English, and markedly upper-class drawl would unexpectedly soften with the slightest of Greek accents on the odd word, rendering it one of the sexiest voices she had ever heard.

'Am I to take it you don't wish to tell me where your husband is?' enquired Niko, his tall, statuesque form gliding past Lindy's desk and to the window behind her.

'I really do wish you'd call me Lindy.' She sighed involuntarily, and was immediately cursing both herself, for inviting yet another glacial rebuff, and Tim Russell for never being around when he was needed.

And where on earth *was* Tim? she wondered irritably. He had sloped off early yesterday afternoon and, as far as she knew, hadn't set foot inside the hotel since—a fact which, coupled with last night's abnormally oppressive heat, had guaranteed her a virtually sleepless night.

5

'Yes, I suppose I should—under the circumstances,' murmured Niko in that soft, drawling voice of his as he parted the slats of the blind to peer out into the dazzle beyond, where sea and skies merged into a single shimmering blue.

'I beg your pardon?' croaked Lindy, scarcely able to believe her ears.

She swivelled round her chair in order to see him, a small frown creasing her brow as her eyes caught sight of the still-livid scar running from within the gleaming black of his hairline right down to the elegant arch of his right eyebrow. Though admitting it brought her a decided pang of guilt, she realised that she found something almost comforting in the sight of that one blemish on the otherwise chiselled perfection of his features—no one had any right to look as good as this man did.

'Perhaps it *is* best if I start calling you by your first name,' he reiterated, his gaze still on the view beyond the window.

Lindy's eyes rolled heavenwards. What was she supposed to do—get down on her knees and thank him for the favour he was bestowing on her? He might be the most gorgeous-looking man she had ever clapped eyes on, but his downright arrogance more than cancelled that out! From the moment he had arrived he had treated both herself and Tim to a brand of polite disdain that left neither of them in any doubt as to who was the master and who the servants.

'And you may call me Niko.'

Had the chair not been of the solid, figure-hugging variety Lindy felt sure she would have fallen from it in shock.

'You've obviously misunderstood me,' she managed coolly. 'I wasn't implying I wanted to be on first-name terms with you...it's just that...well, to be honest, it makes me feel ancient when people refer to me as Mrs Russell.' And nine times out of ten she failed to respond to that bogus name, she added miserably to herself—there having been nothing in the least honest in her stammered excuse.

'Under the circumstances,' murmured Niko, turning from the window to face her, 'it would be rather ludicrous for us to be on anything other than first-name terms.'

Lindy leaned back against the chair, willing herself not to react to the taunting tone of those words and willing her eyes to keep their appreciation to themselves as they surveyed the broad-shouldered muscularity of the body beneath the heavy white silk of the shirt encasing it.

'You keep saying "under the circumstances",' she muttered, hastily removing her unreliable eyes from the muscled tautness of the well-shaped thighs they were now graphically envisaging beneath close-fitting, immaculately tailored black trousers.

'True—I keep saying "under the circumstances",' he concurred, taking a couple of unexpected strides towards her and hauling her to her feet. 'And almost every time you look at me your eyes begin eating me,' he added inconsequentially, his fingers biting painfully into her flesh.

Momentarily stunned by the complete unexpectedness of both his actions and words, Lindy gazed up blankly into the face now scant inches from her own, her wide-spaced blue eyes widening in shock as they discovered just how cold brown eyes could be, even brown ones flecked with gold, as she now discovered his to be, and which should rightly have been the embodiment of nothing but warmth.

'I'm afraid you suffer from a seriously over-inflated ego, Mr Leandros,' Lindy informed him with all the coolness she could muster, given that her pulses seemed intent on breaking the sound barrier. 'Because what you've seen in my eyes and misread is pity—pure and simple! Though I'm sure that, given time, the terrible disfigurement on your head will fade to little more than a barely noticeable scar.'

Had her own common sense not already told her how utterly pathetic that spur of the moment excuse had been the expression of amused disbelief flickering across Niko Leandros's handsome features would have quickly brought it home to her.

'My, my—so you're compassionate as well as beautiful,' he drawled, his words husky with laughter as he sank his fingers none too gently into the shoulder-length thickness of her sun-streaked dark blonde hair and tilted back her head. 'Perhaps I'm a far luckier man than I'd realised.'

'Would you mind letting go of me, Mr Leandros?' demanded Lindy frigidly, his taunting reference to her looks touching a raw nerve in her that put a merciful break on her racing pulses.

'Why? Surely you don't object to a man—even one as grossly disfigured as I am—telling you that you're beautiful?' he enquired silkily, an openly predatory gleam in his eyes as he tugged her body against his.

'I'm not beautiful—and we both know it!' she exclaimed in a strangled voice, tearing her body free from its electrifying contact with his and racing round to the other side of the desk.

'Well, that's a novel line, I must admit,' he muttered, his eyes narrowing to watchful slits as Lindy, her cheeks burning with humiliation, gazed sightlessly down at the papers strewn across the desk.

This was it, she told herself furiously; Tim Russell could rant and rave and make all the threats he liked—she had had enough and was taking the first boat she could get off this damned island!

'Unfortunately for you, I don't find it in the least intriguing when women start playing silly games and fishing for compliments—so you can dispense with both,' he informed her coldly, then added with mocking amusement, 'Under the circumstances, it would pay you to do both with alacrity.'

Lindy's eyes flew to his, anger darkening their blue to navy.

'It seems your husband hasn't had the guts to put you in the picture,' he continued, his eyes taking almost insultingly candid stock of the slim, golden-skinned figure across the desk from him and lingering openly on the softly rounded curves that even the shapeless T-shirt dress she was wearing couldn't disguise. 'Though I can't say I'm surprised—one can't really expect honour in such a man, now, can one?'

'One hasn't the faintest idea what you're talking about,' snapped Lindy, wondering what on earth it was that Tim had been up to this time, and wondering even more at her own perverseness in finding this loathsomely arrogant specimen of a man so unspeakably attractive.

'Really? Not only does he play cards badly and way beyond his means—but he also cheats.'

Lindy only just managed to stifle a groan of complete exasperation. She had had more than enough of Tim Russell and his ghastly ways—even though she had no one to blame but herself for that unpleasant fact.

'Perhaps you will find it a little ironic that, even cheating unchallenged, he still managed to lose you to me last night.'

'What Tim does...' Lindy froze suddenly. 'What did you say?' she just about managed to croak.

'I've just told you that I won you in a poker game last night,' he informed her indifferently, turning and strolling to the door. He paused as he reached it. 'By the way, when your husband turns up—tell him he's fired. I did mention it to him last night, but he was probably too worse the wear for drink to remember... I dare say the fact that his wife is now mine to enjoy has also slipped his memory, so perhaps you'd be good enough to remind him of that too. And, by the way— I've had your things moved into my suite.'

Lindy leaned back against the desk as the door closed behind him, her mind reeling in a daze of confusion. Unconsciously she raised a hand to rub against her upper arm where the imprint of Niko's fingers still tingled against her flesh, while the thought crept accusingly into her head that it was the inexplicable potency of the attraction she felt towards Niko that had somehow prevented her having a show-down with Tim.

Frowning, she shook her head. It was completely irrational of her to feel even a single twinge of guilt. A platonic relationship was what she and Tim had agreed on while they were here—Tim because he was still nursing wounds from a particularly hurtful relationship, and she because... Her thoughts stalled uncertainly. Because, to be perfectly frank, she seemed to have a problem where men were concerned, she told herself bluntly. At fifteen she had lost her heart to the local Romeo, whose callous remarks about her adolescent podginess—which had clung to her with relentless tenacity until she was almost twenty—had left her with a cripplingly negative self-consciousness towards her appearance. Despite the claims of her beautiful mother and her equally stunningly beautiful sister, Joanna, seven years her senior, that such a period of fatness was no more than an unfortunate family trait, she had protected herself so assiduously from the potentially hurtful attentions of males that, when they had eventually begun determinedly seeking her out, her total lack of even the most basic of experience had brought complications she had never even dreamed of to her life. Which was why, she reasoned ruefully, she had welcomed the allegedly broken-hearted Tim so wholeheartedly into her chaotic life. Tim hadn't drooled with what she considered to be the blatant insincerity of other men, she remembered, and—until he had shown his true colours here—neither had he tried to lure her into his bed, the sole aim, she had become convinced, of just about every man with whom she had been coming into contact.

'A year or so out of the London rat race—that's what I need, and what I honestly think you could do with too,' was how Tim had first introduced the subject. 'There's a job going on one of the Greek Islands, managing a super de luxe hotel, which I thought I'd try for... Interested?'

'Very,' Lindy had laughed, 'except that I know absolutely nothing about hotel management.'

'No problem—I know enough for the two of us.'

She realised now that she hadn't really taken his suggestion that she should join him seriously, because her first thought had been how she would miss his availability as an escort whenever she needed one—an escort she could trust not to start making physical overtures as the evening progressed. But she had encouraged him in seeking the job, she reminded herself, her face clouding as she remembered to what extent...even then, the signs were there, she thought angrily—if only she had had the sense to read them. But it was her own pig-headed stubbornness that had been her downfall and led her to all this, she reminded herself harshly. The more sceptical her friends had become, the more protective she had felt towards Tim.

'Lindy, don't be so naïve!' they had chorused. 'He *has* to be expecting a darn sight more than friendship from you, carting you off to some remote Greek island for a year—especially when he's told them all you're his wife!'

'How many times do I have to explain that was a misunderstanding?' she had protested—and one she hadn't been in the least happy to hear of. 'It wasn't until he'd got the job that Tim realised it was for a married couple.'

'Yet he was the only one traipsing back and forth to Greece for interviews,' it had been pointed out to her with such open scepticism that she hadn't dared admit even to her closest friends that it had been her money— her entire savings, in fact—that had financed those trips.

His excuse for borrowing from her had, at the time, been plausible enough, but nothing could alter the fact that he had made no attempt to repay her to date.

Lindy moved from the desk to the window, half closing her eyes against the glare of the sun as she opened the blind. She had closed her ears to the advice of good friends because she had felt sorry for Tim and because she had always yearned for travel and adventure, and this job on Skivos had promised both.

But the gentle—and, to be ruthlessly honest, slightly pathetic—Tim with whom she had arrived had gradually disappeared. In his place had appeared an unpredictably moody, unrecognisably different person against whom she had, soon after their arrival, had to lock her bedroom door of the suite they shared. And she was now beginning to wonder if his tale of a broken heart had been simply that—a tale calculated to breach the defences she had erected against men.

She gave a sudden shrug of dismissal—it didn't really matter because, whatever way she looked at it, she had been well and truly deceived and it was her own stupid fault. The real Tim Russell was bad-tempered, drank far too much and was a womaniser. She paused for an instant before adding gambler and cheat to her list of his attributes, then rolled her eyes in exasperated disbelief. And now he had lost her in a game of poker, she added further to that list before beginning to chuckle weakly as her irrepressible sense of humour belatedly sprang to life and got the better of her.

She reached up and closed the blind, her amusement faltering as a picture of the man to whom she had been lost leapt to her mind... a man who had stirred such strangely primitive feelings within her that they had distracted her from giving her problems with Tim the attention they most certainly warranted; powerful and conflicting feelings of excitement and apprehension that had been laying siege to her right from the very first moment she had caught sight of him.

Without even pausing to knock, Lindy flung open the door to the palatial suite of rooms Niko Leandros occupied on the top floor of the building.

'Where are you?' she demanded, marching straight into the centre of the almost spartan elegance of the drawing-room.

'If it's me you're looking for—I'm here,' drawled Niko's voice from behind her.

Lindy spun round, the angry words she had been about to hurl at him dying on her lips as she caught sight of him.

He was standing in an archway leading off the large room, aggressive masculinity managing to ooze from his every pore, despite the expression of mild boredom

adorning his handsome features. His hair was tousled
and damp, threatening almost to curl against his head,
and the whiteness of the walls and the short towelling
robe encasing his tall, athletic body served only to ac-
centuate the golden sheen of his skin and the hirsute
darkness of his long, perfectly proportioned legs.

The sight of him, even fully clad, was usually enough
to knock the breath from her, Lindy admitted to herself
with fatalistic candour, but it was the sight of his legs
that now froze the anger in her—or, to be precise, the
sight of his right leg, down the outer side of which, from
as much of its thigh as was visible right down almost to
his calf, ran livid, knotted scar tissue.

'There's more, if you're interested,' he murmured
mockingly, his hands moving to the belt of his robe as
his eyes noted the path of hers. 'Though I feel it only
fair to warn you that this is all I'm wearing.'

'I'm perfectly aware that convalescence can be a very
boring time for some people, especially those used to
active lives, Mr Leandros——'

'Niko—I thought we'd agreed.'

'All right—Niko,' ground out Lindy from between
clenched teeth, the anger stifled in her by the sight of
that terrible scar swiftly rekindling. 'But I'd be grateful
if you'd stop trying to amuse yourself at my expense.
And you can start by moving my things back into my
room—I mean, Tim's and my suite.'

She stood her ground as he began walking across the
mottled marble of the floor towards her, determined to
conceal the feeling of intimidation now joining the
morass of other sensations assailing her. He drew to a
halt scarcely a foot from her at the moment when her
nerve was about to desert her completely.

'No, your things will not be moved,' he informed her,
the sudden darkening in his eyes as they met hers cre-

ating a jangling mixture of fear and excitement within her that held her rooted to the spot. 'But yes, I shall be amusing myself at your expense. You see, my golden-haired Lindy, it's quite some time since I've had a woman,' he declared, his eyes boldly proprietorial as they swept the contours of her body.

'Had?' she squeaked, fear all but wiping excitement out of existence in her. This certainly wasn't the type of adventure she had been seeking in coming to this island!

'Had the pleasure of a beautiful woman's company,' he amended with blatant insincerity.

'I know for a fact that's a lie!' retorted Lindy incautiously. 'Women have been coming to this island in their droves ever since you arrived—and every single one of them stunning!'

'Yes, but they're too easy,' he countered lightly. 'They're not as discerning as you are—they all see me as just as beautiful as they are...whereas you see me as disfigured and worthy only of your pity.'

'Niko, honestly, I——' She felt her teeth jar with the sudden force with which she clamped her mouth shut. This was a subject over which she was far too sensitive, she warned herself angrily; she knew perfectly well he was merely amusing himself at her expense, yet she had just been on the verge of trying to console him with the fact that she found his looks little short of perfect!

'No—don't try to salve my pride, Lindy,' he murmured with mocking innocence. 'You can't imagine how intriguing I find it to come across a woman repulsed by my marred looks.'

'Oh, for heaven's sake, I didn't mean to imply I found you repulsive!' she blurted out spontaneously, and immediately regretted her outraged forcefulness. 'Well, not really,' she added, desperately seeking a face-saving balance, but all too aware that she had not succeeded.

'Don't worry,' he murmured, reaching out with both hands to clasp her head, his fingers twining into her hair. 'The challenge you present excites me more than you can imagine.'

With his fingers now playing in blatant sensuality in her hair, and with the fresh after-shower aroma of him bombarding her senses, Lindy was having more than a little difficulty concentrating on his words. She was having considerable difficulty concentrating on anything. She was as good as in his arms, she thought dazedly—all she had to do was raise her own, now hanging limply at her sides, and she would be in the embrace of the most exciting, most desirable...

'I've always been a firm believer in the saying "beauty is only skin deep",' he continued, his words cutting off the torrid meandering of her thoughts.

'So have I,' she agreed in strangled tones—the ugly duckling in a family as good-looking as hers tended to set great store by such sayings.

'And, as you've only seen me in my present unfortunate state, you'll just have to take my word for it that women used to find my looks irresistible before my accident.'

Lindy's eyes flew to his, filled with suspicion. He had to be joking—hadn't he?

'I see what difficulty you're having in believing how incredibly beautiful I once was,' he murmured, his facial expression and his tone equally deadpan.

It was the infinitesimal chance that he actually might be serious that made her pause to take stock before verbally tearing into him. He was Greek, she reminded herself, and from what she had heard Greek men were a pretty macho lot... but one thing she had never heard of was a macho man describing himself as beautiful! Ah—but she had heard something of his having an

English mother... or was it grandmother? She let out an involuntary groan of pure exasperation with herself. Since when were Englishmen given to extolling their own physical attributes so extravagantly? Any fool would have accepted immediately that he was joking at her expense!

'And that's what I find so exhilaratingly novel about all this,' he murmured, the now open caress of his fingers in her hair and the huskiness entering his tone scattering her angry indignation and reawakening the throb of excitement in her with a heady vengeance. 'Knowing that, when you decide to give yourself to me, it won't be because you're dazzled by my pretty face, but because——'

'When I *what*?' shrieked Lindy, her sudden and violent attempt to escape curtailed as his hands slid from her hair to her shoulders and clamped her into immobility.

'Lindy, I realise that the mere idea of your making love with a man as grossly disfigured as I am——'

'You're not disfigured and you damn well know it!' she accused angrily. 'And you also know damn well that you can probably have any woman who takes your fancy!'

'Including you?'

'That's not what I meant!' she groaned in exasperation. 'Damn it——'

'That's the third time in succession you've just sworn,' he snapped, suddenly jerking her body closer to his. 'And I don't like my women swearing.'

'I'm *not* one of your women, and, anyway, "damn" isn't swearing!'

'Yes, you are, and yes, it is, as far as I'm concerned. And, believe you me, you're more mine than any other woman I can think of—you're the first I've owned outright, thanks to the turn of a card.'

'Don't be so ridiculous, you can't *own* a person!' she exclaimed witheringly. 'Slavery was abolished some time back—or hadn't you heard?'

'Well, I've just reinstated it on this island, which I happen to own—or hadn't *you* heard?'

He was laughing as he spoke, displaying strong white and, needless to say, perfect teeth as he did so. And his hands had begun sliding slowly down from her shoulders and were now caressing her back in a way that was affecting both her mind and body quite disastrously.

'But all that's completely irrelevant,' he whispered seductively, drawing her body another fraction closer while stopping short of actual contact. 'You see, I'm not the sort of man who would ever dream of forcing his attentions on a woman.'

Hardly something for him to be boasting about, thought Lindy fuzzily, her head swimming with the almost unbearable tension of the excitement gripping her—the problem was far more likely to be one of women forcing their attentions on him.

'And, of course, you'll have your own bedroom in this suite until such time as you start sharing my bed— a time which will come only when you choose.'

'If that's the case, that time will never come,' retorted Lindy, trotting out the words in which she had little or no faith simply because she felt the occasion demanded them, and also because they afforded her a few seconds' distraction from the overwhelming effect his nearness was having on her.

'Perhaps I'll remind you of those words when you come, eager and impatient, to my arms ... or perhaps then I'll be too distracted even to recall them.'

'Stop it,' she pleaded, the words coming out in a high-pitched squeak that dismayed her.

'Of course I'll stop,' he placated her, while at the same time his head lowered to hers. 'But first I should like to kiss you.'

'Why?' she squeaked inanely, and emitted an even stranger sound as she attempted to clear her throat.

'Because I'd like to; perversely, perhaps, given that I know you'll derive no pleasure whatever from it. But, as I say, there's nothing I enjoy more than a challenge, and your lack of response now will make the passion I shall soon taste on your lips all the sweeter.'

It was then that he drew her fully into his arms, and then that her own rose instinctively to cling around him. Her immediate reaction was of disappointment, and one she instantly transformed into a more acceptable feeling of surprise. It was the unexpected chasteness of his kiss that she found so disconcerting and that made her realise just how terrified she had been of how she might respond. Almost light-headed with relief at finding her fears ungrounded, she felt her rigid muscles relax as the crippling tension that had gripped her for so long swiftly left her. And it was then that he made his move; his arms sliding down her body, his touch electrifying as he moulded her to him, his lips parting hers till his tongue gained entry to plunder and explore the melting guilelessness of her mouth.

And it was in that one fatal moment of relaxation that his body began dictating with impunity to hers; inflaming it into a violence of response far more powerful than anything she had feared. So totally attuned had her body instantly become to his that the urgent swiftness with which potent desire leapt in him neither shocked nor alarmed her. From the start there had been a primitive instinct within her, something that had tried to warn her of what this man was capable of awakening in her and which she was capable of comprehending only when it was too late. But now her body was singing out in reckless joy, marvelling in its magical ability to evoke so unbridled and powerful a response in his.

When, without so much as an instant of warning, he wrenched her from his arms and strode across the room to the huge plate-glass doors leading out to the balcony her reaction was one of such profound disorientation that the only thing she was even vaguely aware of was the sound of her own laboured breathing rasping in her ears.

'Well, as I said,' his disembodied and only marginally breathless voice came to her, 'the next time you'll enjoy it . . . perhaps a little more.'

The sarcasm oozing from his every syllable brought the stinging heat of humiliation crawling over her body. Never in her entire twenty-three years had she experienced anything like this . . . anything as utterly degrading as this! She had allowed herself to be manipulated by an experienced man of the world and had actually thought she was affecting him as devastatingly as he was her!

Anyone would have thought she had never been kissed before! But she had, and with some men had thoroughly enjoyed it . . . yet never once had she come close to losing control of herself, and nothing she had ever experienced could have prepared her for what had happened to her just now.

She raised her hands and pressed them against her burning cheeks as the sickening thought occurred to her that it wasn't even a question of having *allowed* herself to be manipulated by him . . . she had been nothing more than putty in his hands.

'My, my, don't tell me you found kissing me so nauseating that you're incapable of speech,' he taunted.

'Never mind, there's always next time to look forward to.'

'Don't bank on it!' she flung at him in childish despair, then, wishing she had had the sense to keep her mouth shut and simply leave, she turned and walked from the room, tears of rage and humiliation stinging her eyes as the sound of his mocking laughter floated softly to her ears.

CHAPTER TWO

'JUST where the hell have you been?' demanded Lindy, her aggressive words bringing Niko's complaint about her language flashing back to her as she confronted Tim Russell on opening the door to the office.

'Close the door,' he ordered sharply, glancing furtively past her.

'I have every intention of closing it,' she retorted, slamming the door hard behind her. 'Because I don't intend the guests hearing the earful I intend letting you have, you low-down creep! I——'

'I suggest you shut up and listen to what I have to say, because I've only a few minutes.'

'What do you mean—you've only a few minutes?' she demanded, her eyes sweeping contemptuously over his bleary-eyed, ill-shaven features. 'You'll just——'

'It means I've a boatman waiting to take me off this damned island,' he informed her, crouching down to the holdall at his feet and closing it.

Lindy's eyes widened in startled disbelief. In the two months she had been here, as his petty moodiness had hardened to vindictive hectoring and she had lost all memory of the man she had once believed him to be, she had grown to despise him. As for his qualifications for the job, she had yet to puzzle out whether he was very good at hotel management or simply adept at delegating most things, as he invariably did, to the highly trained staff at his disposal. Her friends had been right in their belief that he was expecting more from her than he had admitted, and she recognised his unpleasant behaviour towards her as his way of trying to punish her for so naïvely having believed him—behaviour she responded to with open contempt. This vindictive specimen of manhood she could handle with ease, she told herself, but Niko Leandros was another matter altogether, and for that reason Tim Russell was going nowhere without her!

'Right—let's go,' she stated, anger searing through her as he began laughing derisively. 'If you're worried about honouring your gambling debts I suggest you send Mr Leandros a fiver when we get back to England—that should just about cover my worth, shouldn't it?'

'If I'd known Leandros was likely to be part of it I'd never have got involved in that particular card school,' he muttered, rising to his feet and hooking the holdall over his shoulder. 'Unfortunately I'd had a bit too much to drink by the time he put in his unexpected appearance.'

'Oh, I see. You were drunk, and that makes it perfectly all right for me to be left to the mercies of a self-opinionated playboy, is that it?'

'Who do you think you're kidding, Lindy?' he jeered. 'You fancy him like mad and make no effort to hide it— a fact that makes me see red when I think of the "I wish men would leave me alone" routine you've been dishing out to me. But I'd say Leandros can't exactly be described as impervious to you, as he's the one who suggested I stake you.'

'And how many of you were there in this card game?' demanded Lindy frigidly, refusing even to acknowledge his opening gibes. 'Tell me, Tim, how many other of the degenerate gambling fraternity had the opportunity to win me?'

'He bought the rest of them out of the game—it was just the two of us.' His gaze hardened visibly. 'Damn it,

Lindy, none of this would have happened if you'd behaved like a normal woman towards me. And don't try telling me you expected things to carry on between us as they had in England, because even I refuse to believe you could be that stupid!'

'Sorry to disappoint you,' she rounded on him, trying desperately not to lose her temper, 'but that's exactly what I believed—and what you led me to believe. And to blame me for your bouts of drunkenness, your womanising and your——'

'I hate to interrupt this litany of praise,' he snapped, 'but I really have to get a move on.'

'*We* have to get a move on,' she informed him coldly.

'I'm afraid you're going nowhere while Leandros has your passport.'

Lindy's eyes flew to the safe, in which her passport should have been, uncertainty mixed with horror filling them.

'Sorry, but Leandros insisted on sending one of his henchmen back here for it as a sort of bond,' explained Tim with no discernible trace of remorse.

'I don't believe you,' she croaked weakly. 'My God, you really are the most loathsome apology for a man I've ever had the misfortune to come across!'

He gave a harsh laugh. 'And how would you describe the dashing young Leandros heir?' he sneered. 'I'm sure you'll be only too willing to drop your virginal airs where he's concerned and wheedle your way——'

'I shan't need to wheedle,' she informed him, her words hoarse with disgust. 'Because I intend going to him right this minute and telling him the truth.'

'Oh, yes?' he enquired, his expression mocking. 'You fancy a spell in a Greek gaol, do you? Because that's where he'd have the two of us slapped, make no mistake about that.'

'We haven't broken any laws!' exclaimed Lindy, thrown by a momentary flash of fear darting through her. 'None that could warrant gaol, anyway,' she added uncertainly.

'You have some experience with Greek law, have you?' he sneered, then paused as though savouring an idea. 'Mind you, if the pair of us ended up inside perhaps I'd get an uninterrupted chance to show you exactly the lines along which I'd planned our relationship to develop... though I can no longer guarantee my intentions would be as honourable as they once were.' He smiled wolfishly, hitching the holdall more securely on his shoulder as he did so. 'So yes, why don't you go ahead and confide all in Leandros? It might just have some very interesting repercussions.'

'Get out of here!' she spat at him, trembling with rage, yet startled to detect fear flashing through her once more.

'Yes—I suppose I should, if that's your answer.' He sighed with false regret. 'And I really shouldn't keep that boatman waiting, even though I am paying him a small fortune to get me discreetly over to the mainland... your entire share of our salary, in fact. But I'm sure that, if you play your cards better than I did with Leandros, money won't be one of your worries—the guy's loaded.'

He had actually managed to frighten her with his talk of prison, she admitted bemusedly to herself as the door closed behind him and silence began filling the room with an almost palpable oppressiveness. She frowned, trying to examine that fleeting, puzzling fear, only to find it had disappeared along with the loathsome Tim. Her frown deepened as she remembered how her friends had tried to warn her of how naïve she was being where Tim was concerned. She gave a small shudder as she wondered what their reaction would be to the way things had now turned out—not one of them, she was certain, would have envisaged anything remotely as bad as this. How could she have been so incredibly pig-headed?

'With embarrassing ease,' she gloomily answered herself aloud, suddenly acutely conscious of how completely bereft she was of someone to confide in. Her status as the manager's wife had erected an intangible barrier between herself and the rest of the staff, most of whom spoke quite good English and were unanimously friendly—but it was a friendliness that stopped short of allowing her to seek the actual friendship someone of her open and outgoing nature would naturally have sought. And she had to admit that it had troubled her, she thought unhappily, gazing around the room and frowning suddenly as her attention was caught by the unusual dimness of the light.

She turned and looked behind her, her gaze falling on the graceful marble-pillared lampstand in the corner, the single source lighting the room. She walked over to it, her frown deepening as she removed the heavy manila file balanced on top of the shade which had so dimmed the amount of light being emitted. So, she pondered, mystified and wary, Tim had been sneaking around almost in the dark—obviously intent on slipping in and out unnoticed.

After a few moments' bemused thought she gave a dismissive shrug and tossed the file on to one of the cabinets, gazing around her once more in the now improved light. One thing was for sure, she thought wryly: she wouldn't be taking on the little amount of work Tim hadn't managed to delegate—her lack of Greek ensured that. In fact, though she had found plenty to do in the way of work to keep herself occupied, there had been few specific duties for her to perform. At first, Tim had taken delight in delegating menial tasks to her whenever an opportunity had arisen, though his pleasure had soon diminished with the unconcerned enthusiasm with which she would turn her hand even to something as dull as making beds.

But what was she to do now he was gone? she wondered apprehensively... Her job, non-existent though it was, had been part and parcel of his.

But what was very much more to the point... what was she going to do right now?

Pulling a small face, she switched off the lamp and stumbled her way in the dark to the door—trying to comfort herself with imagining Tim Russell barking his shins on the furniture as he had made the same journey in reverse.

She took the lift to the top floor, her heart thudding painfully in her chest and her thoughts drifting everywhere except to the man she was about to face once more. Had Tim taken only the holdall he had been carrying, or had he had his other things stashed away, ready for a speedy departure? She managed to keep her mind on similarly dredged-up thoughts until the lift doors had opened, knowing that the answers didn't interest her in the least.

Resisting a strong urge to step back into the lift and ride up and down in it all night if it came to it, she strode to the door of Niko's suite and knocked loudly on it before she had a chance to weaken.

'It was unlocked anyway,' he informed her as he opened the door. 'In future, all you have to do is walk in.'

'How was I to know that?' she demanded icily, allowing her eyes to rise no higher than his silk-shirted shoulder-line as she stepped inside. 'Which is my room?'

'I'll take you to it,' he murmured, his face coming disconcertingly into her line of vision as he gave a small, mocking bow. 'I don't suppose your errant husband has turned up, has he?' he asked as he led her through an archway and down a corridor, his words bringing a startled flush of guilt to her face.

'I've really no idea,' she muttered, her words sounding alarmingly strained and reluctant to her ears.

He drew to a halt outside one of the panelled oak doors leading off the corridor.

'When did you last see him?' he asked, turning to face her.

Lindy had begun lowering her eyes the moment they had spotted him turning. 'I can't remember,' she lied, without the slightest glimmer of hope of being believed. 'After what he's done to me, I honestly wouldn't care if I never saw him again!'

'And I doubt very much whether you will—at least, not on this island,' he murmured, his shrewdly watchful eyes never once leaving her face.

'Good,' muttered Lindy. 'Now—is this my room?'

She took a step towards the door outside which they had stopped and found her path blocked by the bulk of his body.

'How long have you been married?'

Lindy bit back an exclamation of irritation, yet as she did so she also experienced the niggling beginnings of alarm. She should have prepared herself for this, she thought nervously. The need for her and Tim to provide any details of their alleged marriage had never arisen, and they had never really discussed concocting any. If she started lying off the top of her head in her present state of tense exhaustion she knew she was perfectly capable of forgetting every lie she had uttered come tomorrow…detailed lying had never been her forte, even at the best of times.

'If you don't mind, I'd rather we didn't even mention the man's name,' she said, striving to sound blasé.

She flinched as his hands descended on her shoulders, and promptly closed her eyes—simply because she couldn't trust them not to betray her one way or another.

'Russell stated in his application form that you were getting married around the middle of August. Given that we're now approaching November, I can't honestly say your attitude reflects that expected of a bride of just over two months.'

With considerable difficulty Lindy forced her mind not to dwell on this further evidence of Tim's calculating duplicity.

'If you already knew—why did you ask?' she snapped, then, realising that that sort of retort would get her nowhere, added hastily, 'If you must know, I married Tim on the rebound.'

She felt like awarding herself a medal for such a gratifying display of mental dexterity.

'Really? Yet you and Russell applied for the job in the spring—I was under the impression that marriages on the rebound took place within a matter of days rather than months.'

'Well, you were wrong,' Lindy retorted, still not daring to open her eyes—especially not now that the faint yet distinctive aroma that was so unmistakably his had started working its way past her nostrils and into her senses. It was a smell that was no more than the vague fragrance of freshly laundered silk, combined with a delicate spiciness, far too subtle to be aftershave—yet it was a smell that was exclusively his and which now seemed to have the power to affect her like a seductive caress.

'Lindy, if you insist on standing here with your eyes closed I shall only kiss you.'

She opened her eyes, not as quickly as she had intended simply because they had reacted to her efforts as

though held together by glue. By the time they were fully
open his features were a blur before them and her lips
were already unconsciously parting to savour the impact
of his.

Her arms reached out to embrace him as her mouth
leapt to eager life beneath the intoxicating ministrations
of his. But it was only her hands that made contact with
his silk-shirted torso, and as she attempted to draw
nearer, her arms straining to encircle him, realisation
slowly began penetrating the fog of excited confusion
clouding her mind that she was being deliberately held
at arm's length. And it was that belatedly dawning realisation that stung her into finding the strength to break
free. What she found doubly humiliating was that he
made no effort to stop her, merely lifting his hands from
her shoulders as she twisted away from him, and it was
with considerable difficulty that she restrained herself
from burying her face in her hands in utter mortification.

'It's not fair,' she panted hoarsely in an attempt to
salvage at least a shred of her tattered pride. 'You're
taking advantage of me when I'm practically dead on
my feet with nervous exhaustion!'

'Why on earth should you be in a state of nervous
exhaustion?' he asked, his tone amused as he opened
the door, then swung her round and propelled her
through it. 'Surely not over that husband of yours, whose
name you don't even wish to hear?'

'No doubt you find this all highly amusing,' she flung
at him, then found herself having to stifle an exclamation of sheer delight as the room was suddenly bathed
in soft light.

It was a large room, airy and uncluttered, and with
delicate splashes of buttery yellow here and there
warming the dazzling whiteness of it. As in the main
living area, this room had an outer wall consisting en-

tirely of huge plate-glass sliding doors, one of which was opened to let the soft night breezes billow and dance through the curtains now drawn across them.

In the middle of the room was a huge canopied bed, its crocheted cotton covering so exquisitely worked that it was as though the bed had been shrouded in dazzling white lace.

Suddenly aware that she was being watched, Lindy brought the infatuated rovings of her eyes to an abrupt halt.

'Why should I find any of this in the least amusing?' he enquired, as though prompting her to continue her onslaught.

'Because you're not a poor defenceless woman who's been used as a poker chip—that's why!' she instantly obliged, anger flashing in her eyes as she spun round to face him. 'You wouldn't find it nearly amusing if you were me, I can assure you!'

The expression on his face proclaimed all too clearly his undoubted amusement and the struggle he was having concealing it, which made her suspect that her 'poor defenceless woman' claim might have been overdoing it a little.

'If I happened to be you I suspect I'd be thanking my lucky stars I'd been won by a man with whom I'm so obviously sexually compatible.'

Lindy was stunned into stupefied silence...she couldn't possibly have heard him correctly!

'And I'd be shuddering at the thought of all the other men who could have won me—none of them, admittedly, as grossly disfigured as I am, but several of them old enough to be your grandfather.'

'You liar! You——' She bit back the words with a ferocity that could have amputated her tongue. She had just been about to let slip she knew it had been a game between himself and Tim alone!

'You were saying?' he drawled, the anger blazing in his eyes a startling contrast to the total lack of expression on his face.

'I was saying you were a liar,' croaked Lindy, suddenly very frightened. 'You . . . you wouldn't be thinking any of those things if you were me, you'd just be terrified and . . . and nervously exhausted,' she finished off lamely.

'I'd say you were the liar,' he informed her in chillingly quiet tones, 'because you're not in the least terrified of me . . . something that could turn out to be a dangerous error of judgement on your part.' He turned and walked to the door. 'There are some matters I should like to discuss with you later, so I'll have food brought up for us in half an hour and I shall expect you to join me then. There's a bathroom leading off the dressing-room—and, if there's anything you find you need, just ask and it will be provided.'

His head dropped in the most minimal of bows before he closed the door behind him.

That bow was typical of him, thought Lindy dazedly, taking leaden steps towards the bed; it was the sort of gesture that only the super-confident—and usually abundantly wealthy—could afford to make. In the lowly, a bow was an act of obeisance—in men such as Niko Leandros it was a none too subtle statement of their feelings of total superiority.

She gazed down at the bed, on which she had been about to sit, and decided its coverings were far too grand for such treatment; instead she made her way over to the dainty gondola chair in front of the dressing-table and sat down.

The sight of her own possessions neatly arranged before her sent a small *frisson* of alarmed awareness winging through her. She opened a couple of the drawers and again found her own possessions neatly stacked inside.

With a groaned sigh she propped her elbows on the dressing-table top, cupping her chin in her hands and gazing despondently at her reflection. Her hair was a mess, she noted half-heartedly—but the streaks of sun in it and the tan she had acquired definitely suited her, she realised with a twinge of surprise. She straightened, picking up a hairbrush and trying to bring some order to her hair.

Suddenly she flung down the hairbrush—was she completely out of her mind? She must be, to be sitting here, twittering away to herself about her appearance and behaving like some sort of concubine in a gilded cage. She shook her head furiously, as though trying to dispel the confusing mixture of emotions the very thought was evoking in her, then glanced down at her watch and leapt to her feet.

Niko Leandros might have a few matters to discuss with her—but so had she one or two she intended discussing with him!

She made a rapid examination of her surroundings and found her rather meagre wardrobe hung neatly away in a spacious dressing-room. What summer clothes she had were several years old and looking decidedly shapeless, but, having lent Tim all her money, she had had no option but to make do with them. She had actually had hopes of a shopping spree in Athens once he had paid her back, she reminded herself resentfully—a resentment that somehow struck her as peculiarly mild, given the mind-boggling thoroughness with which he had deceived her. Probably because she now had so much else to occupy her mind, she decided somewhat irrationally as she entered the bathroom.

Ruthlessly closing her mind to the breathtaking opulence of her surroundings as she took her bath, she concentrated on what she would say to Niko. It was pointless going over the top and frightening herself with thoughts of concubines, she told herself firmly. Moving her into his apartment like this obviously had to be some sort of warped joke on his part, she reasoned calmly—a joke directed at Tim, who was no longer around to respond to it.

'...you're not in the least terrified of me...something that could turn out to be a dangerous error of judgement on your part.'

With those words ringing in her ears, she leapt from the bath and began drying herself vigorously. And, despite the glow of warmth burnishing her skin, she felt herself shiver as she remembered Tim's claim that Niko would be quite likely to have the pair of them slapped in gaol.

'Damn you, Tim Russell!' she groaned frustratedly into a huge, fluffy white towel.

The chances were that Tim had only said that to frighten her...and he had succeeded. And there was no getting away from the fact that Niko Leandros too had frightened her—something for which she should be thankful, because now there was no way she would be tempted to risk telling him the truth.

She entered the dressing-room, a luxury she had heard of but never before experienced, and began riffling through her clothes, vague plans beginning to form in her mind. She would simply suggest that, as Tim was gone...

'For heaven's sake, Lindy, you're not supposed to *know* he's gone!' she groaned aloud. What she would simply suggest was that *if* he was right, and Tim *had* gone, she would work whatever notice was required of her and then return to England.

It was only when she had finished dressing that she became aware of the almost obsessive care she had taken over it—and it was an awareness that had an acutely depressing effect on her already flagging spirits.

She might as well accept the fact that she was attracted to Niko Leandros in a way she had never been attracted to any other man, she told herself despondently. And another fact she might as well face, she informed herself ruthlessly, was that, even had they met under the most ideal of circumstances, he wouldn't have given her even so much as a passing glance.

Having notched the belt of her sea-blue dress as far as it would go, she then dragged her fingers angrily through her hair and undid all the painstaking taming to which she had so assiduously subjected it.

Niko was nowhere to be seen when she reached the drawing-room, and she was gazing anxiously around, wondering if the apartment included a dining-room, when he stepped through the gently billowing curtains now drawn across the balcony doors.

'I usually eat outside,' he announced, his eyes flickering over her in a manner Lindy found deflatingly non-committal.

And obviously he had no intention of making any concession to her preferences, she thought, having to force her legs to do the necessary to propel her across the room. Because her preference would have been to eat under the stars anyway she began dredging her mind for some other aspect of him with which to find fault ... and came up with nothing. It was just that he was the most disgustingly attractive man imaginable, she admitted defeatedly, giving up refusing to acknowledge the painfully breathtaking surge of excitement that had started up in her at the mere sight of him and which seemed to be getting worse the nearer she drew to him.

'I had no idea what you like to eat,' he said, holding aside the curtain for her as she stepped out on to the balcony. 'So I asked for a selection of dishes you've shown a preference for to be sent up.'

He drew out a chair, on which Lindy seated herself with all the aplomb she could muster—which was precious little, given that her every instinct was to cry out in childlike wonderment at the perfection of her surroundings.

The balcony was large and paved with jewel-like mosaics: huge earthenware and marble urns spilled out a profusion of flowering plants, the delicate scents of which had mingled to float in the air with a softly heady fragrance.

The white pedestal table at which she was seated was set for two, crystal wine goblets and heavy silver cutlery glittering and gleaming in the soft light cast by clusters of candles in marble holders of varying heights and positioned in such a way as to enable the two diners to face one another, unimpeded by their presence. To the side of the table was a white trolley, on which sat several silver-canopied dishes and a napkin-wrapped opened bottle of red wine.

'The chef seemed to have no knowledge of your preferences in wine,' he said, taking the seat opposite her, 'so I selected something that should blend in with your culinary tastes...though I wouldn't necessarily bet money on that,' he murmured drily, reaching over and removing the covers from some of the dishes.

Unsettled by his tone, Lindy glanced nervously across the table at him. He was laughing at her, she thought uncomfortably, suddenly acutely conscious of how com-

pletely out of her depth she was in such exotic surroundings and in such sophisticated company.

'It's just that you have such...how can I put
it?...unusual tastes in Greek food,' he murmured, obviously having intercepted her look of discomfort and
feeling obliged to offer a token panacea. 'Anyway, do
help yourself.'

Feeling about as at ease as a peasant might, having
been invited to dine at a king's table, Lindy helped herself
to small portions from a few of the dishes. Her tastes
in Greek food probably did add up to the equivalent of
steak and kidney pie and custard, she thought self-
consciously, but that was only because she had never
had anyone to guide her. In a fit of petty vindictiveness
soon after their arrival Tim had informed her she was
not to mingle with the guests, so she had only twice eaten
in the hotel's superb dining-room. She had taken to
selecting her meals from whatever took her fancy in the
kitchen—the cosy, paternalistic chef giving her little
tasters from one dish or another and often chuckling
with undisguised mirth at the selections she made...had
he been able to speak even a few words of English he
would no doubt have explained what he had so fre-
quently found amusing about her selections. Far from
finding her ignorance amusing, Niko Leandros plainly
found it repellently primitive!

'I'm sorry—I've been unforgivably rude,' he said,
cutting across her mortified thoughts and startling her
with the genuine contrition in his tone. 'Greek food isn't
necessarily to everyone's taste.'

'Oh, but I love it!' exclaimed Lindy. 'It's just
that...well, anyway...I enjoy the dishes I've tried very
much.'

'It's just that what?' he probed, frowning when she
explained her sorties into the kitchen. 'I can't under-

stand why you haven't been eating in the dining-room,'
he said. 'There you'd have been served conventionally
balanced meals.'

'I . . . I just preferred not to,' she stammered.

Every time she opened her mouth she seemed to be
stepping into a potential minefield, she thought wearily,
wondering how long it would be before she tripped
herself up irrevocably.

It wasn't the most relaxed of meals she had ever par-
ticipated in, and certainly not in the remotest way romantic, despite the fairy-tale surroundings and her
princely companion . . . probably because of him, she
thought morosely, for her Adonis of a companion had
lapsed into a decidedly uncompanionable silence which
had lasted throughout a meal patently not to his taste.

It was when two of the waiters arrived to clear things
away and place a tray of coffee inside for them that Lindy
began to see things with a troubling clarity. She began
wondering what the waiters were making of all this—
the manager nowhere to be seen, and his wife now en-
sconced in the private suite of a member of the Leandros
family. The only shred of consolation she managed to
derive from her tortured thoughts was that true
friendship with any other member of staff had been
denied her . . . and that was hardly any consolation at all,
because all she wanted to do was curl up and die from
the humiliation of it all.

'Are you familiar with Greek coffee?' he asked, having
escorted her inside as the waiters had bustled out and
now reaching over to pour the coffee.

Lindy nodded. 'Though I'm afraid I learned the hard
way,' she admitted, remembering the mouthful of coffee
grounds she had almost swallowed as she had attempted
to drain that first cup she had sampled—needless to say,

Tim hadn't warned her and had been waiting for her to do just that.

He smiled as he handed her a cup, a smile that turned her heart over violently, then filled it with an aching sadness as it suddenly recognised this man's total unattainability.

'Mr Leandros——' she broke off as he pulled a comically protesting face and felt the sadness embed itself deeper into her heart '—Niko,' she conceded with the ghost of a smile, 'if...if you're right and Tim doesn't show up——'

'I'd say the likelihood of his showing up is extremely remote now—wouldn't you?' he enquired, his eyes, usually so alert and watchful, trained on the coffee-cup in his hand.

'Yes...well, what I was going to say was that...well, naturally I'd work whatever notice is required of me...and then I'd like to go home.'

'I have no idea what is required of you contractually; I'd guess the contact was solely with your husband and you were no more than an appendage—my late uncle tended to have a pretty chauvinistic attitude to women.'

'Your late uncle?' queried Lindy, having difficulty remaining civil; the very idea of any woman, let alone herself, being regarded as an inconsequential appendage to a man made her see red.

'Yes—late,' he snapped. 'He was the member of the family—a great-uncle, to be precise—who owned this island and, thereby, the hotel.'

'And he must have died recently... I'm sorry to hear that,' muttered Lindy, offering her condolences more out of politeness than any feeling they would be appreciated.

'You knew him?' he drawled.

'You know I didn't,' she replied, her hands clenching in fury in her lap.

'I can't say I did either,' he startled her by admitting.
'One of his eccentricities—of which he had many—was
to have as little to do with his relatives as possible. He
used to take off whenever any member of the family
showed up here.'

Lindy made no reply, though it did occur to her that
regarding it as perfectly normal to win a woman in a
game of poker would probably be described by most as
an example of outright eccentricity.

'Unfortunately I was incapacitated shortly after his
death, and the family's financial advisers decided to go
ahead and find a replacement for the management team
already here but due to leave in August. Personally I'd
simply have wound down the entire operation then and
there—a hotel geared solely to being a holiday haven
throughout the year to a couple of dozen exceptionally
wealthy clients is an anachronism in this day and age.'

'Perhaps it's just as well for the staff that you didn't
have a say in the matter,' retorted Lindy. 'Because they'd
all be out of jobs.'

'Ah, yes,' he murmured sarcastically, 'that abundant
compassion of yours leaps once more to the fore. The
fact is that I have rather a large say in all matters—since
I'm the one the old boy left all this to.'

Mentally kicking herself for having walked straight
into such a put-down, Lindy picked up her cup and took
a mouthful from it—a mouthful, as it turned out, mainly
of coffee grounds. Praying the floor would open up and
swallow her, she was reduced to spitting what she could
back into her cup and hating her companion, who simply
stared at her in disdainful silence for several seconds,
before leaping to his feet and leaving the room.

It served him right for mixing with someone he found
so painfully his inferior, she thought angrily, running
her tongue over her clogged teeth and feeling slightly

nauseous as she succeeded only in spreading the grounds more evenly.

'Here, rinse out your mouth with this,' ordered Niko, returning to shove a glass of water under her nose.

Lindy took a mouthful and washed it around.

'Now—spit it into this,' he instructed with barely concealed impatience, handing her the coffee-cup into which she had already spat once.

'I'm perfectly capable of rinsing out my mouth without you standing over me and giving me blow-by-blow instructions!' she exclaimed irritably once she had obeyed, deciding to put up with the residual grounds in her mouth rather than go through that humiliating performance again. 'To get back to what we were discussing,' she continued as he returned to his seat and resumed drinking his own coffee, 'if you own this damned——'

'Spare me the adjectives,' he drawled languidly.

Resisting an almost overwhelming urge to pick up the coffee-pot and brain him with it, Lindy took a deep breath and started again.

'If you own this hotel, surely whatever you say goes?'

'Yes.'

'So—whether or not I work notice before leaving is entirely up to you.'

'Yes.'

Lindy waited, confidently expecting him to say more. Gradually it dawned on her that she was in for an exceptionally long wait.

'So?' she prompted with reckless aggression. This time her vain wait lasted mere seconds before she made another try. 'So when may I leave?'

'You may *not* leave,' he replied. 'I won you and you're now mine—remember?'

'*Nobody* owns me!' shrieked Lindy, her control snapping as she leapt to her feet. 'And nobody ever will!

I realise that gambling debts are regarded as sacrosanct among hardened gamblers such as you—so, if you would be good enough to let me know how much it is that Tim Russell owes you, I'll see about getting it repaid.'

'Tim Russell?' he queried, batting his eyelids with their profusion of outrageously long lashes at her in a parody of surprise. 'What an extremely odd way for a bride to refer to her husband—even one married on the rebound.'

'How much does he owe you?' Lindy almost screamed at him.

'He owes me nothing,' he replied, smiling as he tilted his head to look up at her, arrogant self-assurance oozing from his every pore. 'He had something I wanted . . . and now it's mine.'

Knowing she would end up gibbering if she didn't get a grip on herself, Lindy took a ragged breath before speaking.

'Mr Leandros—though I know none of the details, I do know that you were involved in a very serious accident.'

'Which ruined my once legendary looks,' he sighed theatrically, the mocking look accompanying his words bringing her blood instantly back to the boiling-point.

'And I realise how difficult convalescence must be for someone as used to the jet-setting social scene as you so obviously are,' she continued through noticeably clenched teeth. 'I realise too——'

'Being a woman of such compassion,' he slipped in mockingly.

'—that you're the type who finds it next to impossible to exist without his playthings,' Lindy ploughed on determinedly. 'So I suggest that you have a selection of them sent here—instead of trying to rope me in as a substitute. Because, as you've already witnessed for yourself tonight, I'd make an absolutely abysmal substitute for the type of women you're used to.'

CHAPTER THREE

BY THE time her eyes had finally begun drooping with the sleep that had so long eluded her, Lindy was already frustratedly aware that her normal waking time was little over an hour away.

She awoke at twenty minutes past eleven and spent several minutes gazing in groggy disbelief at her watch, convinced that there was something wrong with it.

She was showered and dressed within fifteen minutes of waking, her bemused mind still fretting over the lateness of the hour instead of accepting how painfully little sleep she had had during the past two nights.

Two uniformed security guards barred her entrance to the office as she arrived there, her limbs leaden and her temples throbbing with a vicious headache, shaking their heads implacably as she tried to pass them.

Eventually one of the guards opened the door and called to whoever was inside. A few seconds later Niko appeared at the door, his expression grim.

'Yes?' he barked, his eyes contemptuously dismissive as they took in her slightly dishevelled appearance.

'These men seem unwilling to let me into the office,' she explained, annoyed to feel the colour rising hotly in her cheeks.

'They're following my instructions,' he informed her brusquely. 'You no longer work here.' As he uttered those last words he turned back into the room.

'Does that mean I can leave?' she called after him defiantly.

'Whether or not you'll be leaving remains to be seen,' he replied without turning to face her. 'But, if you do, it certainly won't be for England.'

He hadn't even had to raise his voice for the threat in his words to reach her and make her blood run suddenly cold, and it was with an almost sickening feeling of apprehension that she returned down the corridor and out into the sunlit spaciousness of the foyer, the fear within her shadowy and undefined.

'These men are asking to speak to Mr Russell,' Maria, one of the receptionists, called over to her as she arrived.

Lindy walked towards the two men standing at the reception desk.

'I'm afraid Tim—Mr Russell—isn't here,' she apologised.

One of the men immediately began addressing her in rapid Greek.

'I'm very sorry, but I don't speak Greek,' she said, while the second of the men rounded on the Greek girl.

Though she couldn't understand a single word of what was being said, she could tell by their tone and demeanour that neither man was in the least happy, something they were conveying to the startled receptionist in no uncertain terms.

'Maria, what on earth was all that about?' she asked, her heart thudding with alarm as one of the two men now walking towards the door gave her a grim-faced backward glance.

The dark-haired girl glanced quickly around her before leaning discreetly towards Lindy, her eyes eloquent with shocked sympathy.

'Mr Russell owes them money,' she whispered. 'And also to a friend of theirs.'

Lindy leaned weakly against the marbled desk, the thought scurrying through her mind that she couldn't take much more of this.

'Gambling?' she asked in a tight, strained voice.

Maria nodded. 'Those men are from the mainland—and they're the sort who will keep coming back until they've been paid.' Again she glanced around her before leaning even closer towards Lindy. 'This morning the security men came from the bank to collect the receipts.'

'Oh, heck!' groaned Lindy. With Tim away yesterday, none of the necessary cashing up would have been done! 'I'd better go and see to it.'

The Greek girl placed a gently restraining hand on Lindy's arm, shaking her head vigorously as she did so.

'The money has all gone,' she whispered urgently. 'I overheard Mr Niko talking to the head barman...I know they weren't aware I could hear them.'

Dazed and ghostly pale from shock, Lindy tried desperately to assimilate what her mind was equally desperately attempting to reject.

'I...I...' She shook her head in a reflex attempt to clear it. 'Don't worry, I promise I shan't say a word about your having told me,' she vowed hoarsely, patting the girl's hand to give emphasis to her promise before turning and walking, as though in a trance, towards the lift.

Her movements like those of an automaton, she went to her room, changed into a brief black bikini and then belted her beach robe securely around her. On her way back down in the lift the thought occurred to her that it might have been wiser to slip out by a back entrance, but she had dismissed the thought with a small shrug of indifference by the time the lift had deposited her once more in the foyer. Her need for time on her own, time away from people and complete isolation from their sounds, was one no one on this earth was going to deprive her of. Marching straight through the foyer in total oblivion of Maria and the startled glance the girl gave her, Lindy headed for the sea.

She made her way through the tranquil order of the gardens and down the winding, gently sloping steps to the beach. She had discovered the beach on the day of her arrival and had visited it almost daily ever since. Because it was an area rarely used by the guests—the younger ones usually taking off to the more remote islands in the motor launches provided and their elders content to meander through the extensive grounds or play bridge in the peaceful coolness of one of the hotel's many recreation-rooms—this small, idyllic stretch of golden sand had become her own private haven.

Kicking off her mules and slipping out of her robe, she made her way to the water's edge, the soothing sensation of the jewel-like waters of the Aegean Sea lapping around her slim, tanned legs lulling her into almost believing that this was a day no different from any other. And, despite everything, she had been inexplicably happy here. It was hardly a job and it would lead her nowhere from a career point of view—but then, neither had the temping she had been doing in London while optimistically waiting for her dream job to present itself. Yet, in spite of her rude awakening to Tim's true nature and the cringing embarrassment that realisation of her own blind stubbornness had brought her, being here had, more often than not, been like an interlude of almost cleansing peacefulness in her life and one she would never have imagined herself appreciating until she had begun experiencing it.

She had come here with the muddled idea in her head of seeking adventure and had found peace, she thought, then tensed at the sound of her own derisive laughter as reality returned to shatter her brief illusion of peace.

She flung herself into the inviting waters, striking out boldly for a rock about half a mile out to sea, which from the shore had the incongruous appearance of a basking whale. One thing she had always had total confidence in was her ability as a swimmer; in fact, in the years when she had felt fat and totally forsaken, it had been perfecting her swimming into which she had thrown all her youthful energies.

The rock had been much further away than she had judged it, she realised as she at last approached it, and she decided to haul herself up on it and rest before making her way back.

It was as she drew near the rock that she felt several conflicting currents beginning to tug at her. Treading water in an attempt to judge which way she was being carried and from which angle it would be best to approach, she felt herself suddenly sucked down in the water. Every nerve in her geared towards not panicking, she forced her body not to struggle, convinced she would be carried back up to the surface. Still willing herself not to panic, but aware that she was being dragged down even deeper, she opened her eyes and saw that she was being sucked towards a large crevice in the rock.

Her lungs bursting, she allowed herself to be carried along, planning to catch hold of the rock once she reached it and lever herself up. Just as she reached out to gain a hold, the current altered with a stunning viciousness, twisting her body and dragging her head-first against the rock with sickening impact. Her mind became a swirling jumble of pain-filled blackness that began to subside only several agonised minutes later when the rasping sound of her starved lungs replenishing themselves revived a degree of awareness in her. She was draped awkwardly across a ridge of rock—what had looked so smooth and inviting from the shore, she now discovered, was ridged and cratered, and with nowhere, other than where she now hung, that would accommodate a body. She gazed down into the Swiss-cheese effect of the crater in the centre of the rock, the realisation that it was this odd formation that had caused such dangerous turbulence coming to her almost in the same instant as did the searing pain throbbing through her head. And again it was her instincts that took over, dragging her pain-racked body that fraction more securely up on to the ridge before consciousness slipped from her.

A sound, that of a high-speed powerful engine, drifted lazily across her mind. Later that sound was joined by another, a voice that was calling her name and then switched to Greek as it was joined by another. With an almost manic determination she tried to ignore all those sounds. It really was too much, her mind protested in plaintive indignation; all she wanted was a bit of sleep, and now these two men had appeared from nowhere and were shattering her peace by hollering at one another at the top of their lungs!

Her indignation turned to outrage as urgent hands were suddenly placed on her body, prodding her, smoothing aside her hair, and generally making a complete nuisance of themselves.

'Lindy—can you hear me? Are you all right?'

Of course she could hear him—he was bellowing right down her ear, she thought irritably, screwing her eyes shut even tighter—an action that sent fireworks exploding through her head.

'Lindy—for God's sake, say something!'

'Go away,' she obliged, but in a voice so unfamiliar that it would have taken little to convince her it wasn't her own.

'Lindy, what the bloody hell do you think you're doing?' lashed out that voice, what little concern there might have been in it now vanished.

'Niko?' Of course it was Niko, she answered herself in silent confusion. 'You're a fine one to accuse me of swearing...' She ran out of breath as her body was suddenly lifted, her cries of protest being joined by a string of expletives that made his original sample sound as innocuous as a shopping list. It was as that litany of oaths switched from English to Greek that their bodies hit the water, and for several moments she struggled in the lock of his arms, desperate to warn him of the treacherous undercurrents. It was when she felt the power surging through his body and propelling them both free that she relaxed and returned with total confidence to her interrupted sleep.

'There's really nothing wrong with me,' she protested to a nameless face during one of her waking bouts.

'Exactly my diagnosis, I'm pleased to say,' replied a soothing male voice. 'We've just had to give you a little something to keep you sleepy during your return journey to Skivos, but you'll be as right as rain, bar a pretty nasty headache, come tomorrow morning.'

Come tomorrow morning, the headache was more an uncomfortable heaviness than actual pain, and she did feel almost as right as rain.

She sat up gingerly in the bed, trying to get her bearings and letting out a gasp of surprise at finding the receptionist seated by the bedside.

'Maria?' she croaked, frowning in confusion.

'Mrs Russell—how do you feel?' smiled the young woman.

'Fine,' replied Lindy, all she could manage as she strove to suppress a shudder of loathing of the form of address she had eventually given up trying to get other members of the staff to drop. 'What on earth are you doing here, Maria?' she added in what she hoped was a more welcoming tone.

'Mr Niko said that we were to keep an eye on you while he was away.'

Lindy's head jerked in alarm, an action that awakened positive areas of pain in its fuzzy heaviness.

'What do you mean—keep an eye on me?' she asked hoarsely, the events of the past couple of days flooding back into her mind with a horrifying clarity. All that money had gone, and with it Tim . . . and she was Tim's alleged wife. And Niko had made no mention whatever to her of the theft! 'Maria?' she pleaded, making a silent vow that there was no way she would allow herself to end up in a gaol—even if it meant her having to swim to the mainland to avoid it!

'Mr Niko wanted to make sure you had recovered properly from your accident.'

How considerate of him, thought Lindy bitterly. He probably thought she would try to escape. In fact, he probably thought she'd been trying to strike out for the mainland when he had found her on that wretched rock . . . an accomplice on the run!

'But he couldn't watch you himself,' continued Maria, oblivious of her charge's melodramatic train of thought, 'because he had to go back for treatment for his leg.'

'His leg?' echoed Lindy, the pain-riddled heaviness in her head now promising to turn into a full-blown headache.

'He hurt his leg—the one that was already damaged in the accident—when he rescued you,' supplied Maria, a note almost of censure in her voice.

Lindy slumped back limply against the pillows, her terrors dissipated. That was the last thing she had expected to hear, she thought weakly, and was immediately assailed by a blast of guilt at the selfishness of her relief—Niko's leg had already been horrifically damaged to start with.

'That was very thoughtful of Mr Niko,' she murmured contritely. 'But there's really no need for anyone to sit with me—I can always ring down if I need anything.'

'If you're sure,' muttered Maria uncertainly, half rising.

'I'm sure,' replied Lindy firmly. All she wanted was to sleep—and not so much to escape from a now pounding headache, but from the guilt cavorting unrestrainedly within her.

'Thank you, that was delicious,' murmured Lindy as the waiter cleared her supper dishes from the table before her.

'What are you doing up?'

Lindy spun round just in time to see Niko close the door behind him, her mouth tightening angrily as he immediately began a conversation with the waiter now joining him at the doorway. That was typical of him, she fumed angrily to herself, flinging an accusing question at her and then launching into a conversation with someone else without even waiting to hear her reply! Yet as she listened to the exchanges of the two men at the door she felt her anger dissolve into gloomy depression. Despite her total unfamiliarity with the language in which they spoke, the relaxed ease between both men was unmistakable, and there was no hint of that barely veiled master-servant aloofness to which she and Tim had been subjected.

'I left instructions that someone was to sit with you,' he barked across the room as he closed the door behind the departing waiter.

'So Maria told me,' snapped Lindy, her anger once again flaring. 'But I'm not a child who needs——'

'I'd say that point was debatable,' he cut across her words coldly. 'But I felt it would be safer to have someone around just in case there were any repercussions from your...accident.'

His pause before uttering that last word was so infinitesimal that Lindy couldn't be absolutely sure it had occurred, and the fact that he had started walking into the room distracted her from any further examination of it. There was a stiff awkwardness about his stride that filled her with the suspicion that he was doing his utmost not to limp—a suspicion that racked her with debilitating guilt.

'It seems my fears were ungrounded—you appear to have recovered remarkably well,' he observed with cool detachment.

'I have,' replied Lindy stiltedly, her every instinct warning her not to remark on the slowness of his tread or the fact that he was so noticeably favouring his damaged leg. 'And I'd like to thank you for all you did,' she added, her eyes wide with alarm as they followed his now virtually limping progress to a wall cabinet, from which he took a balloon glass and poured himself a brandy.

'I shan't offer you anything to drink, just to be on the safe side,' he stated with no acknowledgement of having heard her tentative words of thanks. 'They seem to have pumped rather a lot of sedatives into you yesterday.'

'About yesterday,' Lindy began, then immediately dried up.

'What about yesterday?'

'I . . . I honestly can't find words to express my gratitude,' she stammered. 'I still can't believe I could have behaved so . . . so stupidly.'

'Stupidly?' he enquired, his eyes on the drink in his hand as he tilted his tall body slightly and leaned one shoulder against the wall. 'In what way stupidly?'

There was something in his tone that froze her. When it had crossed her mind earlier that he might have thought she was trying to swim for the mainland she hadn't been *serious* . . . she hadn't for one moment actually believed he could possibly think such a thing!

'Mr Lean—— Niko, yesterday I was feeling rather down and decided to have a good long swim to try to cheer myself up a bit,' she stated quietly. 'My stupidity was, firstly, in misjudging how far I was attempting to swim, and, secondly, in not having the slightest suspicion that the rock might be so formed as to create such terrible currents . . . though, from the water's surface, you have to admit that there's no indication at all of the turmoil beneath.'

He swirled the brandy around in the glass and took a sip of it before speaking.

'As far as I was aware, that rock is a hazard all new staff—and certainly all the guests—are warned about. Not that I've ever heard of anyone being at risk from it before—no doubt because there aren't that many people around stupid enough to attempt the almost two-mile swim reaching it entails!'

'For your information, even a five-mile swim is perfectly within my capabilities,' retorted Lindy, stung by the open contempt in his tone. 'And I could manage ten with very little difficulty,' she added for good measure.

'If that's the case, the mainland's well within your reach,' he observed mockingly, 'it being only eight miles away.'

'For heaven's sake, you can't possibly think that's what I was attempting!' she exclaimed angrily, now almost convinced that was exactly what he was thinking.

'Why on earth would you want to?'

'This is crazy!' she protested hoarsely, devastated to find how close she was to tears.

'Crazy—precisely,' he agreed, draining his glass. 'So why are we discussing it?'

'Because you said... Oh, forget it,' she capitulated wearily, her every shred of concentration now riveted on willing the tears welling infuriatingly in her eyes not to spill over.

'Forget it?' he enquired with a mildness that was paradoxically almost menacing. 'Is that your method of dealing with any problem you encounter—simply to forget it?'

As he spoke he straightened and took a step towards her, his body visibly tensing with the pain his spontaneous action had inflicted on it.

'Of course it isn't,' she protested, a small gasp of horror escaping her as she watched the colour drain slowly from his pain-clenched features. Why on earth did he insist on putting on this ridiculous act, she wondered, the threatened tears vanishing with shock, when he was so obviously in pain?

'You seem remarkably skilled at forgetting to me,' he insisted, beads of perspiration gleaming on his skin as he stubbornly refused to acknowledge the agony now obviously racking him with each step he took towards her.

'I was simply trying to avoid getting into a pointless argument with you,' she stated, reluctantly accepting that

colluding with his macho stubbornness would be far safer
than challenging it. 'And that's why—— Niko!'

All thought of collusion deserting her, she leapt to her
feet, her body bracing spontaneously to serve as a prop
to his, now swaying precariously.

'I'm all right,' he informed her icily from between
clenched teeth, the arm descending heavily across her
shoulders giving complete denial to his claim.

'Of course you're not!' she exclaimed impatiently,
clamping an arm around his waist, her fingers then
scrabbling to find some steadying purchase against the
lean contours of his hip as he tried shifting his weight
away from his damaged leg. 'You're in agony and it's
pointless your trying to spare me by pretending
otherwise!'

'Spare you?' he enquired, the soft drawl of his words
now so close to her that she could feel the softness of
their breath against her hair, sending a sharp tingle of
awareness rippling down her spine. 'What makes you
think I should wish to spare you anything?'

'For heaven's sake, Niko, it's obvious you did further
damage to your leg when you got me off that rock—
any fool could tell that by the way you're limping now!'

'And you're a fool?'

Lindy let out a barely stifled groan, one that was a
mixture of exasperation, frustration and a disruptive
sense of utter confusion. When it came to one-to-one
verbal confrontations with most people she could more
than hold her own—but not with this man. Never before
in her life had she been virtually reduced to the mental
equivalent of jelly by verbal attacks; just as never before
in her life had she been so acutely aware of the physical
presence of a man. And that was probably the crux of
the whole thing, she informed herself despondently. His
mere presence had caused her problems right from the

start, clouding her mind to the extent that she had become incapable of objectivity even towards something as blatantly unacceptable as her relationship with Tim.

And it was difficult enough having to cope with being in the same room with him, she reminded herself agitatedly, let along clinging like a limpet to him as she was now—even if she was doing so only from the purest of motives. But the warmth emanating from his body might just as well have been that of a furnace, given the effect it was having on her, she admitted to herself with mounting alarm; and once again there was that wholesome, barely definable scent of him, permeating her every sense like a powerfully intoxicating drug.

'Take your time, Lindy,' he murmured with a seductive softness that only heightened the chaos within her, his arm no longer there for support as it tightened around her. 'We have the night before us, so don't rush into any decision as to whether or not you consider yourself a fool.'

'My God, what a creep you are! I've never met a more loathsome creature than you in my entire life!' she hurled at him, fighting in a fury of outrage to break free from him. 'You're the most—— Oh, my God, Niko!'

In complete panic, she attempted to revert to propping him up as he suddenly slumped heavily against her. She heard the involuntary groan of pain that escaped him as he tried to twist his body clear of hers when she began falling backwards, and heard the sharp catch of the breath torn from her own lungs as she landed awkwardly on the sofa with him sprawling half on top of her.

'Niko, I'm sorry. . . I really am,' she gasped raggedly, horrified by the starkness of his pallor and the luminous darkness of pain in his eyes as he drew away from her.

And she then found herself even more horrified by the fact that she was having to fight an almost over-whelming urge to reach up to cup his pain-filled face in her hands and warm it back to vitality with the heat from the fire now surging fiercely within her. 'You're in such terrible pain and it's all my fault.'

'And no doubt you intend assuaging that pain as only a woman can,' he muttered, the arm she hadn't even realised was trapped beneath her now moving and drawing her firmly against him. 'Driven, needless to say, by guilt and that boundless compassion with which you're so remarkably blessed.'

'Niko, why do you always have to be so cynical?' she asked sadly, not attempting to draw free from the suf-focating nearness of him, and not even bothering to try convincing herself that her immobility was from a fear of causing his tortured body further pain. 'Why can't you just accept the fact that I'm bound to feel guilty——?'

'And why can't you just accept the fact that the idea of a beautiful woman being in my arms solely from reasons of guilt doesn't appeal to me in the least?' he asked softly, tilting her head back against his shoulder till she had no option, other than closing her eyes, but to meet his gaze. 'And that is the only reason you're in my arms...isn't it?'

Several problems were besieging her all at the one time: there was the considerable difficulty she had in dragging her mind from its orgiastic wallowing in the fact that he had just so casually—so almost convincingly—referred to her as beautiful; then there was the effect being wrought on her by those enigmatic gold-flecked brown eyes now locked with hers...and the ·inconceivable question of what her own might be betraying. If the eyes truly were the mirrors of the soul then hers would have much to betray, she realised with a sudden, sickening clarity. Even in her lonely, romance-starved adolescence, she had never been given to having crushes on pop and film stars, but that was the closest analogy she could come up with for her inexplicable reaction, right from the start, to this disturbingly attractive man. And the reason she was in his arms was because that was where a restless, sensual and completely alien part of her craved to be.

'Lindy, am I to take it from your silence that it isn't guilt that's brought you into my arms?' he asked, an underlying mockery in the softness of his words, while his hand rose to the nape of her neck, where his fingers embarked on idle exploration.

It was that disturbingly tantalising, yet paradoxically almost soothing movement of his fingers against her skin that made her aware of the discomfort in her left arm, trapped behind his body. She moved it, a peculiar, though not in the least unpleasant, weakness wafting through her as she felt the solid warmth of his back beneath the softness of his shirt and realised that the position of comfort into which her arm had automatically slipped was around him.

'Lindy?'

'What?' So much for sophisticated repartee, she thought despondently as the word slipped baldly from her, her eyes suddenly widening in shock as she looked down and found her right hand resting on his thigh. She had absolutely no idea how, or even when, it had come to be there.

'Perhaps it's not so much guilt as pity,' he taunted relentlessly, the play of his fingers ceasing as they sank into her hair and held her head immobile as his own began lowering towards hers. 'And a beautiful woman's pity is probably the most emasculating thing there is to a man,' he continued, his mouth closing over hers in the same instant that he finished uttering those derisive words.

And, though there was a part of her that demanded she resist, it was a part that stood no chance against the alien force within her that leapt in ardent response to the practised seduction of the mouth now goading hers to a hunger she had never before experienced.

'You're a prize even a saint would be tempted to gamble for,' he whispered huskily before his mouth returned to hers in a swift upsurge of passion.

It was the tone of his words that deafened her ears to their contentious content and filled her with a sharp ache of longing. Ardent, yet teasing, his tone had been that almost of a light-hearted lover, and the ache within her warned her that heartfelt words of love were what she might one day crave to hear on this man's lips. It was a warning that shocked her and brought a sharp cry of protest to her lips, but it was a cry that was reduced to a soft moan of acquiescence beneath the impatient ardency of his mouth.

She made to lift her hand from his thigh, the need in her overwhelming to curl her arms tightly around him, and found it trapped in his. For a moment their hands remained motionless, hers sandwiched between his and the muscled tautness of his thigh. Then, exerting no discernible pressure, he began guiding her hand; at first leading it deeper against the muscled hardness of his inner thigh and then drawing it slowly up his body. By the time he had brought it to a rest, sliding it inside the silken softness of his shirt to lie against the hollowed smoothness of his stomach, her entire body had become racked by a quivering devastation of need against a background of suffocating apprehension.

Without uttering a single word, yet with an explicitness she had found as shocking as she had found it electrifyingly arousing, he had left her with no shred of doubt as to the full potency of his desire for her. And, though her mind had been incapable of fully grasping the true impact of the message he had so casually imparted to her, she realised now that that moment had been the most sexually intimate she had ever shared with a man.

As his mouth drew away from hers and lowered to explore with hot moistness against her throat she felt the taut warmth of his stomach muscles against her palm and a trembling urgency rising within her for her hand to retrace the path it had so briefly traversed.

He drew his head from against her, gold glittering hotly in his eyes as he gazed down at her. And then he began laughing softly and, still laughing, undid his shirt, his fingers closing round her tempted, wavering hand.

'Why do you hesitate?' he asked, challenge in his laughing words. 'Perhaps it's only fair for me to warn you that I have no time for sexual coyness.'

Lindy tore free her hand, the ungovernable heat in her extinguished by the mockery in those words.

'And neither do I,' she breathed raggedly through passion-bruised lips. 'It seems my abundant compassion almost got the better of me,' she lied with a bitterness directed almost entirely at herself.

For a moment his body tensed, then a coldly careless smile crept across his lips as he removed his arm from around her and brought it to rest along the back of the sofa.

'That and your remarkable ability to forget... inconsequential things, such as your husband and the fact that, for all you know, he could have disappeared off the face of the earth.'

Lindy leapt to her feet, her cheeks burning.

'Or perhaps I misjudge you...perhaps you do know where he is.'

'I don't,' she protested, her denial ringing out falsely against her ears, even though it had been more or less the truth.

'I must say I find your attitude somewhat intriguing,' he drawled softly, his eyes glittering ice where moments before there had been torrid heat. 'I know you claim to have married the man on the rebound, but surely any normal woman—no matter what her reason for marrying him—would be a little worried by now...after all, he could have met with an accident.'

Lindy glared back into those icy eyes, knowing there was nothing she could say that would condemn her any less than would her silence.

'Well, let me put that compassionate heart of yours at rest,' he mocked, easing himself awkwardly to his feet and offering her a look of contemptuous amusement as she automatically took several steps back from him. 'Lindy, how many times do I have to tell you that I'm simply not the type to force himself on a woman—especially not one as obviously reluctant as you?'

He laughed with open derision as the colour deepened hotly on her cheeks.

'Now, where was I? Ah, yes, your missing husband. You'll no doubt be relieved to hear he's safely off the island—having paid one of the boatmen a ludicrous sum to take him over to the mainland in secrecy.' He began moving slowly and haltingly towards the archway, no longer making any attempt to disguise the damage to his leg. 'Of course, he could afford to chuck money around, it being mine rather than his...part of a fairly considerable sum.' He turned and glanced back at her as he reached the archway. 'How much, exactly, was it that he stole? The figure seems to have slipped my mind.'

'I've no idea,' protested Lindy, her voice cracked and uneven.

'Not down to the last drachma, perhaps,' he stated coldly. 'But the fact that he'd stolen it hasn't exactly come to you as the shock I'd expected it to—now, has it, my oh, so compassionate Lindy?'

Without waiting for any reply she might have made, he disappeared through the archway, leaving Lindy white-faced and despairing and bitterly ruing her own stupidity in ever having even considered accompanying Tim to this island.

CHAPTER FOUR

'So, YOU'VE decided to join me in the pool, have you?'

The sound of those taunting words from behind her brought Lindy to a halt just as she was about to step out through the main door of the suite.

'No, I haven't,' she snapped as she partially regained her composure. By now Niko had usually had his swim and taken himself off to wherever it was he spent most of his days, she thought frustratedly. 'I'm going for a swim in the sea!' she called out defiantly as she stepped through the door and slammed it behind her.

'I've told you I don't want you swimming alone in the sea,' Niko reminded her blandly as his tall tracksuited figure entered the lift behind her before the doors had a chance to respond to her vicious stab at the button that would close them.

'You *told* me no such thing!' retorted Lindy hotly, her hands moving reflexively to check that the lapels of her towelling robe weren't gaping as she caught sight of a large expanse of tanned, profusely haired chest beneath the unzipped jacket of his tracksuit. 'You issued an order forbidding me to put so much as a toe in the sea!'

'Did I really?' he murmured in mock surprise, laughter twinkling in the eyes moving to her hands, still gripping at the lapels of her robe. 'That only goes to show the depths of my concern for your safety.'

Lindy's lips compressed in a tight line of resentment. Her every instinct had been to ignore that arrogantly issued order of his, and it had only been her overriding

guilt at the consequences of her last venture into the sea
that had prevented her from doing so.

'Aren't you just the tiniest bit flattered by such concern
on my part?' he goaded softly. 'There are a few women
I know who certainly would be.'

'I'm sure there are dozens of them,' responded Lindy
scathingly. 'But I don't happen to be one of them. And
I feel I should point out that the only reason I haven't
been swimming in the sea is because I happen to feel
guilty about all the trouble I caused last time—and *not*
because you ordered me not to!'

'But now you obviously no longer feel any such guilt,'
he mocked.

Lindy flashed him a look of pure loathing, even
though she was perfectly aware that she had no one but
herself to blame for having yet again talked herself into
a corner. 'If you must know, I had no intention of
swimming in the sea today,' she retorted defiantly.
'Well . . . not until I realised that you intended swimming
so much later today,' she added with a muddled contradiction that left her fuming with irritation with herself.

'Oh—I see,' murmured, with that false innocence that
only served to irritate her further. He stepped from the
lift as the doors opened. 'I realise the pool's only one-
third Olympic size, but I'm sure that's large enough to
accommodate the two of us.'

He turned, wedging one broad shoulder against a door
to prevent its closure as Lindy held back undecidedly.

She had spent the past four or five days cooped up
on her own, with nothing to do and with no one to talk
to, she thought frustratedly, discounting her now impatiently glowering companion, who was hardly ever
around. She would go out of her mind if she didn't do
something to relieve this unmitigated boredom, she told
herself, then stepped past him out of the lift.

'I simply thought you'd want to swim alone,' she muttered, annoyed to find herself automatically quickening her own stride to keep pace with his as he sauntered past her.

'I don't know why you should think that,' he replied, nodding a greeting to the solitary member of the now much-reduced staff they met on their way to the pool.

'I've watched you a couple of times,' she said, an admission she instantly regretted. 'You seem to be following an intensely rigorous training routine.'

Not simply for a couple of days, but day after day she had watched the statuesque figure, now stripping down beside her, plough its merciless way up and down the pool. Her appreciation of the powerful perfection of his style had been tinged with puzzlement as to why he should suddenly decide to inflict such severe punishment on a body still not wholly recovered from what had obviously been a very serious accident.

'Training routine?' he queried. 'I've merely been swimming up and down the pool—my physiotherapist suggested it as therapy,' he added, kicking free of his tracksuit bottoms.

Lindy's hands faltered at the belt of her robe, her eyes widening in disbelief.

'Has your physiotherapist ever watched you in action in the water?' she asked, a smile creeping involuntarily to her lips.

He shook his head, then tilted it questioningly, the elegant black arch of his left eyebrow rising in query.

'It's just that I doubt if he'd regard as therapeutic the way you plough up and down this pool.'

'Is that so?' he murmured, a predatory gleam entering his eyes as she slipped off her robe. 'I'd have thought most people would realise I'm a man who does nothing by half-measures.'

As he spoke his eyes were taking leisurely account of her body, pausing to linger as they roved before settling with undisguised interest on the golden-skinned swell of her breasts.

'A thought has just occurred to me,' he said, an edge of huskiness entering his voice. 'Perhaps it would have been wiser had I not stripped off like this.'

Lindy was having enough problems with the tight knot of excitement unravelling in the pit of her stomach and snaking its way throughout her to be able to search for any sense in those seemingly nonsensical words he had just uttered. She had somehow got it into her head that, while men were apt to become inflamed by the sight of a female body, the reverse didn't apply, she realised fuzzily. Yet it would take a woman with nothing but ice in her veins to remain unaffected by the bronzed perfection of the body, naked save for a pair of brief black shorts, standing in statuesque stillness beside her.

The softness of his laughter dancing to her ears snapped Lindy out of her almost trance-like reverie.

'Perhaps if you were to try concentrating more on my damaged bits and less on the rest of me your eyes would be less inclined to gobble me up as they're doing right now,' he murmured helpfully, his laughter deepening as she flashed him a look of fury.

'Actually, your leg seems to be healing remarkably well,' managed Lindy, desperate to salvage what scrap she could from this mortifying exchange. She screwed up her eyes, praying that they would convey nothing more than critical detachment as she trained them on a muscled brown leg, every bit as perfectly proportioned as its left counterpart. The extensive scar running down its outer side had lost nearly all its knotted lividity and was fast fading to what would one day be no more than a tell-tale white line. 'Yes, very well indeed,' she added

for good measure, and was relieved to feel what she was
sure were the patches of scarlet on her cheeks subside.

'And to think I was contemplating swimming in
tracksuit bottoms so as not to offend those delicate blue
eyes of yours,' he chuckled. 'Whereas all they've done
is gobble me up, damage and all.' There was the glint
of mockery in his eyes as he reached out and drew a
forefinger lightly across her mouth. 'Soon—very soon,'
he murmured, laughing as she angrily brushed aside his
hand and flung herself into the water.

Though she knew the pool was heated now that the
weather had got cooler, the water felt like ice against the
burning of her flesh as she kicked out into a strong crawl.

Seconds later she felt his body skim the length of hers
beneath the water and was aware of him surfacing several
yards ahead of her, his body instantly powering itself
into the punishing routine to which he had accustomed
it.

He was still ploughing relentlessly up and down the
pool when Lindy decided she had had enough. She had
expended her energies far too quickly by childishly trying
to match his speed when they had first entered the water.
All the same, she felt a lot better for her swim, she told
herself as she reached up her hands to haul herself out
at the side of the pool—refreshed and invigorated.

She was halfway out of the water when her entire body
froze to petrified stillness. She recognised instantly two
of the three men walking purposefully towards the pool
as those who had turned up several days ago, demanding repayment of what Tim owed them. The third,
she supposed with stomach-churning apprehension, must
be their friend to whom Tim was also apparently in debt.

For several agonised moments she contemplated
simply letting go of her grip on the side of the pool and
sinking to oblivion beneath the water. Then, her head

spinning in panic, she irrationally began berating herself
for not even knowing the equivalent of 'go away' in
Greek.

She was still vacillating, now in a complete state of
panic, when she heard Niko's voice call across to the
men from behind her.

This was it, she told herself fatalistically; she would
have to tell Niko everything. Her head shook with a
sudden vehemence as that now almost familiar fear began
niggling in the pit of her stomach.

'Leave us and wait for me up in the suite,' ordered
Niko, heaving his glistening body from the water right
beside her.

'But I can explain!' she blurted out, gazing up at him
with an expression verging on terror.

'I said leave us!' he snapped, turning as he walked
over to join the men.

With her eyes never once straying in the direction of
the four men, Lindy got out of the water, into her robe
and left the pool area.

She raced up to the suite, changed into a dress, then
went to the balcony overlooking the pool, from where
she had so often watched Niko swim. She was trembling
from head to foot as she gazed down at the four men,
now deep in conversation, and, though she was chilled
to the bone, she knew it was fear rather than the cold
that was its cause.

After several minutes of straining her ears to catch
sounds she wouldn't have understood even had she been
able to hear them, she turned her back on the tableau
below and leaned disconsolately against the wrought-iron
balustrading.

She had offered to explain, but the fear crawling within
her told her she could not. She tried to examine that
fear, but found it impossible now that it had returned—

just as she seemed to find it impossible to believe its existence once she was free from it.

'I told you to wait for me in the suite!'

Lindy glanced up at the sound of those snarled words and found Niko's tracksuited figure striding angrily towards her.

She made no move to resist when he grasped her by the wrist and led her to the lift. And in the highly charged silence in which they rode to the suite her entire concentration centred solely on unfreezing the stupefied block into which her mind had retreated.

'Right,' he snarled, turning and slamming her against the suite door he had just hurled closed behind them, 'you and I have things to discuss!'

'Stop bullying me!' screamed Lindy, fury unblocking her frozen mind as she tore herself free and raced to the centre of the room.

'Bullying you?' he demanded harshly, striding after her. 'It's a wonder I didn't drag you up here by the scruff of your neck—or to the police station, which is where you and that criminal of a husband of yours belong!' he snarled, scowling down at her.

Lindy, who had by now fully recovered her mental capacities and had been about to kick out at him, fully prepared to take pot luck as to which of his legs she struck, felt herself freeze.

'Why should I belong with the police just because he does?' she blustered, inwardly crumbling. 'His gambling debts aren't mine.'

'What about his other debts?'

'What other debts?' she croaked, a mounting sense of panic seriously impairing her ability to reason.

'Don't try pretending you don't know who those three men were,' he accused witheringly. 'Nor that that crooked little rat of a husband of yours owes two of them large sums in gambling debts—not to mention the other, who owns a night-club on the mainland.' He broke off with a snort of disgust. 'God only knows how the pair of you managed to run up a tab that size in so short a time!'

Though now feeling totally bemused and demoralised, Lindy forced her eyes to meet the cold accusation in his with a reckless defiance.

'What with the gambling and night-clubbing debts I've just settled, I've parted with an extremely large amount of money,' he informed her coldly. 'The total of which, added to the money your husband stole from this hotel, amounts to a very substantial sum by any standards.'

For one terrible moment Lindy felt she was going to keel over from the shock of what she was hearing. She knew some sort of reaction was expected of her, but her mouth had gone sandpaper-dry on her and her mind seemed to have seized up completely.

'Perhaps you'd be good enough to tell me just how many more people I'm likely to encounter, queuing up for settlement of your and your husband's debts,' he drawled bitingly, fury simmering in the eyes locked with hers.

Lindy struggled to get her mind back into some semblance of a working order, then gave up, closing her eyes and resorting to praying with a childlike fervour for a magic that would erase this moment—or, better still, the past two months.

'Just the roughest of estimates will do,' he murmured with venomous softness.

'I...I sincerely hope there will be none,' she eventually managed hoarsely. 'But I can't honestly say there won't be any.'

'Is there anything you *can* say honestly?' he asked coldly, grasping her by the shoulders and shaking her angrily.

'Yes, there is!' she flung at him, her eyes flying open to blaze with anger as she violently twisted free. Who the hell did he think he was that he had the right to sneer at her as though she were some sort of criminal? 'I'll pay you back! Just you tell me how much of your precious money is involved and, even if it takes me the rest of my life, I'll damned well pay every penny of it back to you! You're the last person on this earth I'd ever want to be indebted to!'

In the silence following that reckless outburst she had plenty of time to think those rash words over and to come to the conclusion that she must be out of her mind.

'Well—how much is it?' she demanded, despite a sickening churning in the pit of her stomach warning her that she was completely and absolutely out of her mind and that the answer was probably the last thing she would want to hear.

The sum he gave her brought her an instant of giddy relief—it was so ludicrous that he could only be joking! One look at his totally humourless features dispelled all trace of that ill-judged relief.

'So, unless you happen to have such a sum stashed away somewhere, I'd say you'll have a decided problem fulfilling such a rash vow,' he informed her with frigid contempt.

'I don't care how, but I'll get it!' she insisted insanely, wondering, even as she uttered the words, why she had bothered wasting her breath on them—the rest of her life would probably provide insufficient time for her to raise an amount like that.

'And how, exactly?' he enquired in that same coldly supercilious tone. 'Though do keep it in mind that you happen to constitute one of the few debts your elusive husband has actually cleared... and that I have no intention whatever of allowing you to take up any form of employment.'

'You're mad!' protested Lindy in outrage. 'It's ridiculous—you can't possibly think you can keep me here against my will... I'll go to the police!'

'I admit that is your only option,' he retorted with a shrug. 'Take it by all means, though the chances are you'll end up staying with the police—or, more accurately, in one of their prisons—for a lot longer than you'd bargained for... for several years, I'd say.'

In that instant an understanding that had till then eluded her flashed into her mind. In the past couple of weeks she had learned things about herself she had hitherto been completely unaware of... but the one she had found impossible to pin down, she now realised, was that there was a latent fear buried within her of being imprisoned that amounted almost to a phobia. It was something she had never given a moment's thought until recently—but then, the likelihood of her ever landing in gaol had been so remote as to have been non-existent... but Tim's mention of prison had triggered that dormant fear within her and given it the power to magnify itself into terror.

'But how will I get the money to pay you back?' she asked in a defeated whisper, torn between her fear and the vow she had so recklessly made.

Surprise flashed into his eyes before they narrowed suddenly and he gave an indifferent shrug.

'As you said—you can't exactly be held responsible for your husband's debts,' he muttered.

'I also said I'd repay you,' she insisted stubbornly, driven by a pride she would gladly have dispensed with had she had the choice. 'And I certainly don't want any favours from you,' she added with a flash of her old spirit.

His eyes roved insolently down her body, then rose in open mockery to hers.

'I think that deep down you're aware of exactly how much you'd enjoy my favours,' he taunted softly, 'especially now that you seem to have overcome your feelings of revulsion towards my marred physical appearance—or perhaps it's only my vanity that led me to think it was desire I was reading in your eyes by the pool.'

There was now something close to loathing in Lindy's eyes as they swept over the magnificently proportioned body before her. He had everything, she thought bitterly, materially as well as physically; and the mockery in the eyes now challenging hers proclaimed his arrogant confidence in both himself and those devastating looks that few women would find possible to resist.

'Have your joke, if you must, Niko,' she flung at him scathingly. 'But I can assure you that you wouldn't find the subject quite so amusing if you'd ever experienced what it was really like to look repulsive.'

'Why, Lindy,' he murmured with blatant insincerity, 'are you actually verbally acknowledging that my looks don't fill you with revulsion?'

'They don't—but your character most certainly does!' she exploded. 'And that's why you're the last person I'd ever want to be indebted to!'

'Are you this passionate between the sheets?' he asked with a chuckle. 'I hope I don't have too long to wait to find out.'

Lindy opened her mouth to hurl whatever abuse came to mind at him, then hesitated, her eyes widening in protest at the idea suddenly entering her head.

'If that's the way you feel, perhaps we could do a deal,' she said in a voice that wasn't in the least steady.

Ruthlessly suppressing the strident cacophony of protest raging within her, she forced her reluctant hands to the top of her button-through, lightweight denim dress.

'How much am I worth, Niko?' she asked, the huskiness of incredulity at her own behaviour in her tone as her shaking fingers worked their way through the buttons. 'Am I worth all that money you've just paid out?'

'Lindy, what do you think you're doing?' he asked, his own tone distinctly wary.

'Displaying the goods, Niko,' she informed him, her voice lacking the note of confidence she would have liked, her mind grappling with the unwelcome vision of her family with which her imagination was presenting her—of her sister and her father convulsed with laughter at the idea of her attempting to play the *femme fatale*; her mother, on the other hand, didn't seem in the least amused as she briskly ordered her to do up her dress and behave herself.

'You're what?' croaked Niko, plainly on the brink of a new experience—that of being at a loss for words.

'For heaven's sake—I asked you how much you thought I was worth!' exclaimed Lindy exasperatedly, racking her mind as to how she should proceed now that all the buttons were undone.

She closed her eyes, took the deepest breath her lungs could contain and began easing the dress off her shoulders.

'Stop this!' roared Niko, his hands rough against her skin as they dragged the dress back over her shoulders. 'Do you honestly think I'd want to have anything to do with a woman who's prepared to prostitute herself like this?'

'How dare you judge me?' raged Lindy, tearing herself free and hugging the dress tightly around her. 'You as good as bought me—so what does that make you?'

For several seconds they faced one another in fury-charged silence, a black scowl of rage on his face as his eyes burned down into the blue eyes glaring fiercely up into his.

'Nothing I have done can condone the way you've just behaved,' he accused harshly.

Lindy blinked, and as she did so something seemed to snap in her and exactly what she had attempted in the blindness of rage hit her with a swift and devastating clarity.

She took a halting step back from him, then a second. She froze for an instant, gazing dazedly around her, then staggered to the sofa and crumpled heavily down on to it.

For several seconds she battled for control, then lowered her head in anguished shame as she felt the tears begin spilling down her cheeks.

'Lindy, stop that at once!' he snarled, striding towards her.

'Do you think I wouldn't if I could?' she shrieked, mortified beyond endurance by what was happening to her. 'Do you honestly think I'd make a fool of myself by choice in front of a loathsome creature like you?'

'You can call me all the childish names you like,' he muttered, the angry snarl gone from his voice. 'And you can cry all you like,' he added, in direct contradiction to his previously snarled order, 'because you're wasting your time... your tears don't have the slightest effect on me.'

Lindy's head lifted, tears and perplexity mingling in her gaze. Whatever his words might claim, his tone told her far more clearly than any words ever could just how positively he was being affected—and in a way he was finding next to impossible to handle.

'Niko?' she choked, his name blurting from her as an almost suffocating tightness leapt to her chest.

His look almost fearful in its wariness, he suddenly lifted both his arms and locked his hands behind his head. Had it been the gesture of a man about to embark on a series of physical exercises it would have been unremarkable. Coming, as it did, from a man who obviously had no such purpose in mind, it suddenly struck Lindy as having all the hallmarks of being the adult equivalent of a small, suddenly disorientated child sticking his thumb in his mouth for comfort.

It was the most crazy in a series of ludicrous thoughts she had had, Lindy told herself angrily as he suddenly lowered his arms, swung round and walked away from her to the huge windows.

When the telephone began ringing he turned once again and walked to the alcove in which it sat.

There was barely any trace of a limp left as he walked now, thought Lindy, doggedly steering her mind away from the disconcerting peculiarity of those past few moments. She concentrated instead on his voice, now uttering their soft, and, to her, completely unintelligible, sounds of Greek into the mouthpiece. After a few moments of it she felt that suffocating tightness grip her once more and she knew that, whatever had happened in those few strange moments—and even if whatever it was had been nothing more than a figment of her often grossly flamboyant imagination—it had alerted her to the knowledge that in Niko Leandros she had met a man she could all too easily love, and love with an intensity that might well prove to be her destruction.

He glanced across at her as he replaced the receiver, a small frown creasing his brow as he saw the deathly pallor now masking her features.

'Perhaps there is a deal we can do, after all,' he stated tonelessly. 'There's a problem I have that your presence here could do a lot to lessen.'

CHAPTER FIVE

'YOU obviously had quite some relationship with this woman, so why can't you just say so?' The unexpected aggression she heard in her voice startled Lindy.

'Do you intend listening to what I'm trying to say,' demanded Niko, 'or do you plan interrupting me all the time with whatever fanciful notion enters your head?'

Lindy's face took on a stubborn look. She was only interrupting because he was making a lot more of whatever it was he had to say than the meal they had just eaten, she objected irritably to herself. And it was freezing out here on the patio!

He had insisted on showering and changing, and their then sharing the late lunch he had ordered. It was only when they had finished lunch, and coffee had been brought to them, still on the chilly patio, that he had finally broached the subject—yet with a reticence that had initially intrigued her and then made her almost certain he had something to hide.

'I just like to get my facts straight,' she muttered defensively, taking a sip of coffee and then drawing her cardigan more tightly around her. At least she had had the sense to put it on, she thought morosely, her spirits sinking further as she remembered the denim dress she had screwed up into a ball and vowed never to so much as look at again.

'You *do* surprise me,' he drawled, reaching over and pouring himself more coffee and seemingly oblivious to the cold wind now scurrying around the balcony.

'Anyway, whatever relationship I had with Arista is over—and thank God, because she'd started getting it into her head that marriage to me would round her life off nicely.'

Lindy's eyebrows rose a fraction; she found it impossible to believe that any woman would regard marriage to a man like Niko Leandros as a means of rounding off her life—nicely or otherwise.

'You obviously have some difficulty envisaging any woman being foolish enough to want to marry me,' he murmured with saccharine sweetness.

Praying that the cold was hiding the colour rising in her cheeks, Lindy shrugged. 'It's more a case of having difficulty envisaging how a woman would contemplate such a thing without an element of encouragement from the man concerned.'

'You'd be surprised what some women can read even into something as innocent as a dinner invitation,' he informed her drily. 'But I've never knowingly given any woman reason to believe I'm interested in such a binding commitment as marriage.'

'How terribly sporting of you,' drawled Lindy acidly—the man was unbelievable! 'Some people call that wanting to have your cake and eat it!'

'All right—I like to have my cake and eat it,' he conceded with a shrug. 'So can we now dispense with all this character analysis and let me get on with what I was saying?'

'By all means,' murmured Lindy, noting with perverse satisfaction the angry tensing of his jaw.

'Anyway, if Arista is as determined to get back into my life as she appears to be, the chances are she'll be as hell-bent as she ever was on getting married.' He broke off to ladle sugar into his coffee and stir it energetically. 'So that's it,' he finished off lamely.

Was it heck, thought Lindy sceptically, now actually beginning to enjoy herself.

'Niko, what I don't quite understand,' she began innocently, 'is why you don't simply tell her she's not welcome to come here. After all, you've just about wound down this place as a hotel.' The question then crossed her mind as to how she and Tim would have stood—his contract was for a year. It was the next question to cross her mind that she voiced with the same slightly cloying innocence. 'And another thing I don't understand is why—as your relationship with this Arista has obviously finished—you just don't tell her you don't wish to start it up again.'

He flashed her a look that revived the realisation in her of exactly how much was at stake for her in all this, and there was hatred in the look she hurled back at him— for the power he had to awaken the spectre of fear in her.

'Are you always this nosy?' he snapped.

'It wasn't my intention to be nosy,' she retorted. 'I just feel I should have some background information so that I don't say or do the wrong thing.' She had heard the tension creep into her voice and had seen the sudden shrewd narrowing of his eyes as he too had detected it. 'Perhaps I did sound nosy,' she conceded, forcing brightness into the words. 'But I dare say you would too if you'd spent days cooped up on your own with no one to talk to.'

'You have me to talk to.'

'You're hardly ever here.'

'I'm around the place,' he murmured vaguely, then added, 'And, of course, I'm here throughout the entire night.'

Lindy had to clamp her lips to suppress a groan of frustration as she felt hot colour flood her cheeks.

'So—when is this woman arriving?' she snapped. 'And what's my role meant to be in all this?'

'Arista arrives the day after tomorrow. And you are the woman with whom . . . let's say, with whom she will find me smitten.'

'Oh, do let's,' muttered Lindy sarcastically, only to receive a positively murderous look as she made to continue. 'For heaven's sake, Niko, how can you possibly expect me to take this seriously and be of any use to you if you refuse to let me ask any relevant questions?' she protested in exasperation.

'It's all perfectly straightforward,' he muttered uncooperatively, 'so why confuse the issue with questions?'

One thing of which Lindy now felt certain was that the issue wasn't in the least straightforward; the Nikos of this world had no difficulty whatsoever in dealing with the sort of problem he was claiming his to be.

'You say you're to appear smitten by me,' she stated coolly. 'That brings several questions to mind: am I to appear similarly smitten by you? If not, how am I to behave towards you? If so, ditto, and am I to be your fiancée or just some passing fancy of yours?'

'Of course you're not to be my fiancée!' he exclaimed, the horror in his tone, which he had made no attempt to conceal, not only infuriating her but bruising her ego to a disconcerting extent. 'And yes, you will return my feelings . . . though that's not to say you're to be in any way familiar towards me, unless I happen to indicate such a necessity to you.'

'Oh—I see,' said Lindy, fury pushing her almost to the verge of collapse. 'I'm to mince after my master— at however many respectful paces behind him he decrees—and, should he require any less docile services from me, he'll no doubt kick me in the solar plexus, or wherever else takes his fancy, in order to activate me!'

Several expressions flitted swiftly across his face, the most prominent of which, to Lindy's astonishment, being amusement.

'I couldn't have put it more succinctly myself,' he murmured, raising his cup to his lips to mask his smile, while at the same time lowering his lids over the laughter almost dancing in his eyes. 'Though I'm sure we can think of a more civilised method of activating you— perhaps a sharp pinch would suffice.'

Lindy picked up her own cup, oblivious to the coldness of the coffee as she pondered uneasily. One moment he had her practically falling off her chair with outrage, and the next he had her almost beguiled by the fact that he happened to possess a sense of humour.

'Well, it's good to have that settled,' he murmured, and moved to rise.

'I beg your pardon?' exclaimed Lindy, dragging her mind back from its discomfiting thoughts.

'I said it's——'

'I know perfectly well what you said,' she snapped impatiently. 'I just can't believe you said it—we've settled nothing!'

'Correct me if I'm wrong,' he ground out, no trace of anything resembling laughter now in his eyes, 'but you did say I was the last person to whom you'd wish to be indebted—yet, when I offer you an opportunity not to be, you turn it down!'

'I haven't turned anything down!' exclaimed Lindy, slumping back against her chair in disbelief. 'You've still told me practically nothing!'

'Simply because there's nothing else to tell,' he muttered irritably.

'Right—so if I happen to say the wrong thing, simply through ignorance, you won't hold it against me?'

'Arista's hardly likely to slap you up against a wall and cross-examine you, for heaven's sake!'

'But what sort of reception can I expect? If I'm likely to be attacked by a jealous woman I should at least be prepared for it.'

The look with which he greeted her words was glacial.

'I'm quite certain Arista is not the sort of woman who would go round brawling with rivals,' he informed her in tones that mirrored his look.

It was the word 'rivals' that did it, thought Lindy, anger and disgust clawing into her. What it really came down to was that this unknown Arista would arrive here with love and hope in her heart, only to find a 'rival' installed. Then she gave a small, confused shake of her head as logic told her that any man capable of that sort of cruelty would also be capable of simply telling the woman concerned that she wasn't welcome in the first place.

'I asked you why you just didn't tell her not to come here,' she said, feeling as though she was going round in ever more confusing circles. 'You still haven't told me.'

'I can't put her off coming here,' he muttered, as though no further explanation could possibly be required of him.

'And why do you need me when she comes here—why can't you simply tell her the truth?'

His eyes met hers, the glimmer of amusement in them.

'Do I really have to spell it out?' he drawled. 'I'm made of the same flesh and blood as any other man, and once she's here...' His shrug was eloquent as his words petered out. 'Arista can be a very desirable woman when she puts her mind to it.'

Lindy's hands clenched tightly in her lap.

'Why don't you simply marry her, if you find her so desirable?' she asked frigidly, unable to believe that earlier she had actually considered herself to be in danger of falling in love with this evil-hearted, calculatingly callous womaniser. 'She's obviously your type, as you got yourself involved with her in the first place,' she continued acidly. 'And, mercifully, she's not the sort to go around attacking her rivals, so, should this overwhelming desire you feel for her happen to wear off, I'm sure you wouldn't have any problem finding yourself a mistress.'

The expression on his face, as he leapt to his feet, was scandalised.

'It goes without saying that your attitude to marriage and mine are not so much a continent apart as an entire world,' he informed her in tones of barely suppressed rage. 'Yet you, who—if you're to be believed—feel that marrying simply from pique is acceptable, have the temerity to feel outrage when I speak honestly about my relationships with women! I have never sought any favour from any woman by holding out the prospect of marriage to her. How I might behave towards a woman I would want to marry I have no idea—simply because I have never met one. But one thing is for certain: if or when I do marry it will be for no reason other than that I have met someone with whom I wish to share my life— *all* of it!' Rage blazing unabated in his eyes, he kicked aside his chair and strode towards the opened plate-glass door, half turning when he reached it and uttering a word in Greek. 'In English it's called love,' he snarled by way of a translation. 'It has yet to enter my life, but I can assure that, should it ever do so, it will be the only mistress I shall ever have!'

Lindy clasped her arms tightly around her, a gesture of reflex misery rather than any acknowledgement of the cold that had now seeped its way through to her bones.

She should have taken up her parents' offer and joined them when they had moved to Edinburgh, she told herself despondently, never having experienced such savage feelings of loneliness and isolation in her life before. She had closed her ears to the advice of her friends because Tim and what he might have proved to be had been irrelevant—what she had come here in search of was adventure...and in her foolishly head-in-the-clouds quest for it had succeeded in landing herself in the most ghastly mess imaginable! Adventure? She was a woman of twenty-three, for heaven's sake!

She closed her eyes as though to close off her thoughts, then immediately opened them to escape the picture of Niko's outraged features that seemed to have become engraved on her mind. However arrogant he might be, however cavalier in his treatment of this Arista, who must surely love him, there could be no doubting the sincerity of his vitriolic outburst concerning love and marriage. And, though they might be poles apart in every other way, his beliefs, in that respect, mirrored her own—that love, when she eventually found it, would be something she would nurture and protect with every fibre of her being and would rejoice in for the rest of her life.

She half rose from her chair, then slumped defeatedly back on to it. Her every instinct was to rush after him and acknowledge his sentiments as her own...but she had no delusions as to what his reaction would be. To him she was the woman who had married a crook on a frivolous rebound...the woman who, from the start, had devoured him with her eyes.

*   *   *

Niko found her the next afternoon, helping one of the few maids left to prepare the sumptuous suite Arista would occupy.

'You are not employed here as a maid,' he informed her coldly from the doorway. 'In fact, you're not employed here in any capacity.'

Her cheeks scarlet, Lindy smiled a sheepish apology to the girl and joined him at the door.

'I was giving a hand because there are so few maids left,' she explained tentatively. 'I mean...now that there aren't any guests——'

'And soon there won't be any staff—that's the way I want it,' he cut in dismissively, his eyes flickering disdainfully over her slim figure. 'I've been looking for you to tell you your wardrobe's arrived—I suggest you sort through it and make sure it's satisfactory.'

He had turned and was walking away down the marbled corridor almost as he uttered his last word. Lindy raced after him, catching up with him by the lift.

'I think I must have misheard you,' she exclaimed breathlessly.

'I said that your wardrobe had arrived,' he enunciated with studiously insulting clarity.

'And what's that supposed to mean, for heaven's sake?'

'It means precisely what it says,' he snapped, stepping into the lift.

'I've enough clothes of my own, thank you very much!' exclaimed Lindy angrily, only just managing to slip in between the closing doors of the lift. This was completely crazy!

'I dare say,' he drawled, his eyes almost reptilian in their coldness as they once again flickered down her body, 'but none of them in the least suitable.'

'Suitable for what?' she enquired, her voice tight with
fury. 'One of your passing fancies?'

His hand snaked out and grabbed a handful of her
particularly baggy knitted cotton dress—one of many in
the same material that had unfortunately returned from
the laundry several sizes larger than they had been orig-
inally—and hauled her against him.

'But isn't that exactly what you are, my scruffy
Aphrodite—one of my passing fancies?'

His lips were on hers, angry and punishing, before she
had any time to react. By the time she had started fighting
him his arms were already closing tightly around her,
trapping in uselessness against his chest the hands attempting frantically to push him from her. He turned to
her, sandwiching her body between his and the wall of
the lift, trapping her head till there was nowhere she
could turn from the bruising punishment of his lips. But
it was through her own hands that her body began betraying her, the wild thudding of his heart beneath her
trapped palms momentarily confusing her with its tu-
multuous rhythm, then sending an answering surge of
excitement lurching hotly through her veins.

'Stop doing this to me,' she begged hoarsely as the
savage onslaught of his mouth fleetingly eased, but they
were words whose tone lacked any of the censure of their
content, and it was with a fiercely uninhibited welcome
that her lips answered the renewed bombardment from
his.

It was some time after the lift had stopped and its
doors had glided open that Lindy became aware of either
fact—and then only because it was more or less pointed
out to her.

'I've a feeling we've arrived...somewhere,' he muttered hoarsely, slowly disengaging his neck from the vice-

like grip of her arms, his movements like those of one
in a trance.

'What do you mean...somewhere?' croaked Lindy,
the question dazed and reflex.

He gazed down at her, the softness of passion re-
ceding swiftly from his features even as his fingers
reached out, almost absent-mindedly, to trace the faintly
swollen contours of her mouth.

'Whatever your game is, Lindy, it could turn out to
be a very dangerous one...and one that I shall end up
deriving far more enjoyment from than you ever could,'
he whispered, a sharp edge of threat in the husky softness
of his words. Then his hand dropped from her mouth
and he turned. 'Come on, we haven't all day. I want to
make sure those clothes will be all right on you.'

Her mind and her body struggling for freedom from
those last vestiges of sensual torpor still clinging to her,
Lindy followed him into the suite, both hating and envying him his ability to switch from passion to coldness
with little more than a momentary falter. Which only
went to show exactly how shallow his emotions were,
she informed herself with the savage bitterness of the
total humiliation now threatening to swamp her. Uttering a muffled cry of rage, she pushed him violently
out of her way and began racing towards her room.

He caught her before she was even halfway down the
corridor.

'Your manners leave a lot to be desired!' he exploded,
spinning her round and slamming her hard against the
wall, his face pale with rage.

'Probably because I don't have the superior breeding
you so obviously have!' she yelled back at him in startled
fury. 'Just who the hell do you think you are?'

'I'm the one calling all the shots! I'm surprised you'd
forgotten,' he flung back at her. 'So I suggest you get

yourself into your room and start trying on those clothes!'

'Go to hell!'

'Lindy, I'm warning you,' he whispered, his jaw clenching as he battled with the fury he was having such manifest difficulty in containing.

'Of what are you warning me?' she demanded, too enraged even to consider the possible consequences of such reckless goading. 'That you'll have me shot at dawn if I don't jump to attention and obey your orders?'

'There's no question of your not obeying my orders,' he informed her harshly, grasping her by the arm and marching her to her room.

'Let go of me!'

'Shut up and do as you're told,' he snarled, opening the door and sending her hurtling into the room.

'Are you out of your mind?' shrieked Lindy, beside herself with fury. 'You have to be to think you can treat anyone the way you're treating me!'

His hand dropped from her arm as though it had been scalded. Then he took a step back from her, his face suddenly shedding all expression.

'Do you honestly think I go around treating normal people the way you goad me into treating you?' he muttered, his words startling her with their almost dazed note of disbelief—an expression she was even more confused to find mirrored in his eyes.

'I *am* normal,' she protested reflexly, but her tone betrayed her confusion and the fact that the fight had suddenly gone out of her too.

'So try on the clothes...please.'

'All right.'

The look he threw her only served to confuse her further in that it mirrored every bit as much uneasiness as she was feeling. They were both volatile people, he probably more so than she; yet at this very moment she knew instinctively and with an unquestioning certainty that the violence that had erupted between them was as alien and disturbing to him as it was to her... but the discomfort they now shared was in the apparent paradox that they were more at ease with one another in battle than they ever could be in the restrained politeness they were now so studiously attempting.

'Good,' he said, giving her a slightly tentative look before closing the door behind him and striding towards the dressing-table. 'It's all there,' he muttered, nodding towards the pile of expensive-looking boxes and carrier bags stacked by the bed. 'So get cracking.'

Finding herself almost welcoming the familiar peremptoriness that had crept into those final words, Lindy decided she must definitely be out of her mind. She watched as he reached for the small gondola chair by the dressing-table and straddled it, her own eyes widening as they suddenly detected the familiar mocking challenge in his.

'You must be joking,' she protested, awareness belatedly dawning on her that he certainly wasn't.

'Lindy, just get on with it,' he drawled, crossing his arms over the back of the chair, his eyes unwavering as he lowered his chin to the cushion of his arms.

Determinedly ignoring the fact that she felt far more at ease now, despite those balefully unwavering eyes, than she had in those awkward moments of politeness, Lindy glared over at him, willing the dainty chair to collapse beneath his weight.

'If you think you're going to get your kicks from watching me strip, you can think again,' she informed him sharply.

'What makes you so sure I'd get any kicks—as you so elegantly put it—out of watching you strip?' he enquired, a smugly evil smile curling on his lips as his ever-watchful eyes spotted the colour rising swiftly to her cheeks. 'And, besides, it's not that long ago that you were hell-bent on stripping for me.'

'Yes, and for my pains you accused me of prostituting myself!' she informed him viciously, all consciousness of those last few disconcerting moments gone as she instinctively retaliated.

For an instant his entire body seemed to freeze as a look of icy fury replaced the smugness of his smile.

'That was completely different,' he snapped, his eyes inexplicably dropping from hers.

'How, exactly?' demanded Lindy, intrigued by how thoroughly her reminder had rattled him—though she couldn't think why it possibly should have.

'I really don't know why we're having this ridiculous conversation,' he parried, his eyes rising once more to hers as he regained his composure. 'Because I don't recall ever having demanded a striptease of you—you're perfectly free to change in the bathroom, if that's what you want...just as long as you try on those damned clothes!'

Lindy turned her attention to the packages by the bed.

'There are enough of them,' she complained as the utter ridiculousness of their even being there returned to niggle at her. 'Did you choose them?' she demanded, her tone accusing.

'Of course I didn't choose the wretched things!' he exclaimed irritably. 'I had a friend take care of it—one whose taste is a darn sight better than yours.'

'A woman friend, no doubt,' snapped Lindy, scowling down at the packages before squatting to gather the whole lot precariously in her arms.

'I'd hardly ask a man to choose them,' his taunting reply came floating after her as she staggered towards the bathroom and sent half the packages flying in ahead of her once she had managed to get the door open. 'Like a hand?'

She gave the door a vicious slam behind her as his mocking laughter danced to her ears, then kicked the box nearest to her in a petulant explosion of frustration.

For a few seconds she toyed with the idea of locking the door and refusing to come out. A wry smile crept to her lips as she wondered how long he would give her before breaking the door down—that he would actually do it she didn't for one moment doubt.

She gave a groaned sigh as she sat down on the marbled floor, her hand reaching out to pick up the russet-coloured blouse that had spilled from the box on which she had just vented part of her frustration. Her eyes widened as her fingers found themselves luxuriating in the opulent heaviness of silk. She closed her eyes as her fingers were suddenly reliving the sensation of a different silk playing beneath them, and beneath that silk the muscled firmness of masculine flesh.

'No!' she protested hoarsely, desperation in the eyes now flying open as she forced her trembling hands towards the packages surrounding her in an effort to distract both her mind and body from the dangerous excitement threatening to overpower them.

Her entire world had been thrown out of kilter; it was as though she was viewing life from an alien and distorted perspective... where she felt more at ease with the violence of the man causing that distortion than she did with his stilted politeness. The desperation deepened in her eyes as she reminded herself that violence was not truly part of Niko's nature—of that she was unwaveringly sure.

She kept telling herself that she was trapped, her thoughts continued in growing dejection, that all she wanted was to escape . . . yet there was a part of her that would willingly remain here on any terms, and it was a part of her that was growing more powerful and demanding with every passing day.

CHAPTER SIX

HER solace in those uncertain years of her adolescence, it was to the water she had once again turned for comfort, Lindy admitted to herself as she dived into the pool. Yesterday she had spent so much time in the water that it had elicited the remark from Niko that she would soon have skin like a prune.

And that unkind remark had been about the sum total of her verbal contact with another human being yesterday—if Niko could actually be counted as a member of the human race, she thought morosely, her slim body flying through the water, fuelled by a desperation of loneliness and futility.

She was trapped in every conceivable way, nagged her relentlessly despondent thoughts: by that initial, seemingly harmless lie that had opened the way to her coming to Skivos and which now threatened to snowball out of all proportion, but most of all she was trapped by Niko—not because of Tim and his almost risible use of her as a poker chip, but because of that ever-growing part of her that seemed to welcome, if not encourage, his keeping her here.

Her body shifted up a gear, skimming furiously through the water. Once men had begun showing such an interest in her it had been to the noticeably self-possessed, mentally strong ones that she had found herself attracted—men who tended to have *ingénues* such as herself for breakfast, she reminded herself with a tinge of wry bitterness. But never towards any of them had she felt anything even approaching the powerful attraction she had towards Niko.

She swam to the edge of the pool and hauled herself out. It was only when she was belting her robe around her that her initial feelings of invigoration deserted her— her legs were feeling a little wobbly beneath her and she was beginning to regret the fury of energy she had just so recklessly expended.

She flung her towel over her head as she entered the lift and rubbed half-heartedly at her wet hair on the journey up. It wasn't the swimming up and down like a lunatic that had left her feeling as drained as this, she told herself bitterly. It was simply an accumulation of all this horrific and unrelieved stress she was under! She felt as though she was being attacked from all sides— and, no matter what front she might have put up to Niko, the impending visit of this woman, Arista, terrified her! It was blatantly obvious that there was far more to it than he was prepared to admit, yet, far from intriguing her, as it had initially, his attitude was now making her edgy and unsure. And the chances were that in this state she would end up making a complete hash of the whole thing—and then where would she be?

'Where the hell have you been?'

'Having my nails manicured!' she almost howled, hurling her sodden towel in angry desperation in the direction of the man scowling across the room at her. 'Where the hell does it look as though I've been?'

'Lindy, I won't have you talking to me in that tone!' he rasped, striding across to her.

'Why not? It's a lot more civilised than the tone you use on me!'

'Lindy——'

'And, just in case you're worried about how I'll behave in front of your excruciatingly important guest, you can rest assured I shall grovel away to you to your heart's content!'

'Spare me that,' he drawled, his eyes narrowing ominously as they swept her bedraggled appearance. 'I'd hate any friend of mine suspecting I'd had a personality change—as I would have had if I appeared with a grovelling half-wit in tow.'

'You surprise me,' retorted Lindy. 'With your attitude to women, I'd have thought a half-witted slave would be the norm for you!'

'I assure you I can be quite amazingly civilised, given the right woman,' he murmured, his eyes flickering over her once more, this time with open disdain. 'But what I really can't abide is a woman slopping around the place, looking a mess. For heaven's sake, go and do something with yourself—your hair in particular!'

'Having second thoughts, Niko?' she taunted, the self-destructive demon in her now openly spoiling for a fight.

'Come into a lot of money, have you, Lindy?' he taunted back. 'Or does the idea of a spell in prison suddenly appeal?'

Pride and fear waging war within her, she glared up at him in silence.

'For heaven's sake, go and have a bath!' he exclaimed impatiently. 'You're turning blue with the cold.' He gave a sudden exasperated shake of his head. 'Lindy, I know you think I nag you simply for the sake of it—but do you really have to stay in the water until you're shrivelled and blue?'

Lindy gazed at him in perplexed silence. There had been a faint note in his tone, almost like grudging affection, and its effect was to kill fear stone dead in her.

'Lindy, for heaven's sake—go and have a bath!'

'Yes, sir,' she clowned, relief dancing through her as she dropped him a small curtsy. 'Anything you say, sir! And as for my hair——'

'Lindy!' he growled warningly.

She turned and fled towards her room, a shriek of shock escaping her as something wet landed against her shoulder.

'You forgot your towel,' his mocking words drifted after her.

She closed the door of her bedroom behind her and slumped weakly against it. Her temper and tongue were her own worst enemies, she reminded herself nervously... and she had just been reminded in no uncertain terms where they could lead her. When she had attacked he had retaliated by reawakening her fears... and then, in the next moment, freed her of them simply by changing his tone.

She was beginning to react like a well-trained circus animal, she informed herself bitterly; and was so appalled by the fact that she fumed furiously to herself over it during her bath and continued to do so while she washed her hair.

Still disturbed, and feeling drained and almost cold after drying her hair, she began dressing, choosing a long-sleeved bottle-green shirt-waister style for warmth. The other day, when virtually forced into trying on these clothes, she hadn't been in the least impressed by any of them, feeling they simply weren't her. Yet now, as she gazed at her reflection, an expression of bemused disbelief began spreading over her face. It was the sort of dress that looked nothing on a hanger and one which she probably wouldn't have given even a second glance... but now that she was in it she felt—almost looked—a million dollars. And an awful lot of money was what it had obviously cost, she thought nervously, quickly skimming through the rest of her newly acquired wardrobe with a more appreciative eye.

Half an hour later, having slipped in and out of several of the outfits, she was back in the green dress and was wondering about the unknown woman with her faultless—not to mention wildly expensive—taste, who had put together such a breathtaking collection of clothes for a complete stranger.

What would really complete the picture, she informed herself wryly as she once more faced herself in the mirror, was a string of emeralds. She chuckled at the thought as she toyed with a ribbon, uncertain whether or not to tie back her hair, then frowned, her expression suddenly mutinous as she scraped its gleaming thickness back into a pony-tail.

'Lindy, I ordered coffee for you, and it'll get cold if you don't come and drink it!' called Niko, hammering loudly at the door. 'And you do realise, don't you, that Arista will be here in about an hour?'

Lindy froze, her hands clenching at her sides. This was ridiculous, she thought as panic welled up in her; she was terrified out of her wits! He could deck her out in all the finery there was, but nothing would alter what she was and the fact that she would stand out like a sore thumb against this woman he found so irresistible!

'Lindy!'

'I'm coming, for heaven's sake!' she yelled before she could bite back the words, racing towards the door and walking smack into it as Niko flung it open. 'You see?' she exclaimed, rubbing her cheek where the door had caught it. 'I become accident-prone whenever I'm nervous, and that's the last thing you need! You'll end up blaming me——'

'Lindy, what on earth are you drivelling on about?' he demanded, dragging her hand away from her cheek and inspecting the damage for himself. 'Are you all right?'

'No, I'm not! I've just told you I'm accident——'

'For heaven's sake, *I'm* the one who flung open the door!'

'Yes, but *I'm* the one who promptly walked into it!'

'Damn it, Lindy, talk sense, will you?' he exclaimed exasperatedly. 'Look—I'm sorry I hit you with the door and I...' He broke off with an exclamation of impatience as she tried to butt in. 'Why don't we just go and have that coffee before it's undrinkable?' he suggested, grabbing her by the hand and dragging her out of the room after him.

Cutting her off each time she made to speak, he led her to the drawing-room and sat her down. Twice more preventing her from saying anything, he poured two coffees and handed her one.

'Right—first of all, is your cheek OK?' he asked, his tone decidedly lacking in sympathy.

'Yes, but——'

'And secondly—before you start raving again—what is it you feel I'm going to blame you for?'

Lindy opened her mouth to reply, then hesitated and took a drink of her coffee instead.

'For heaven's sake!' groaned Niko. 'One minute it's practically impossible to shut you up, and the next you've nothing to say for yourself!'

'I can't think when I'm being browbeaten,' she protested.

'Nobody's browbeating you,' he roared. 'I simply asked you to tell me——'

'I heard what you said!' she cut in angrily. 'And you *are* browbeating me!'

'Well, it wasn't my intention to,' he snapped, flinging himself down on a chair and glowering across at her.

He picked up his coffee-cup and drained it, his look altering to one of wariness.

'Perhaps you'd feel a bit more relaxed if I told you how charming you look in that dress,' he muttered.

'Why on earth should I?' she demanded, outraged. 'And hasn't anyone told you that sarcasm's the lowest form of wit?'

'For God's sake, Lindy, I wasn't being sarcastic!' he groaned. 'What in heaven's name has got into you?'

'As I've tried to tell you, several times, I'm nervous about your girlfriend——'

'Arista is *not* my girlfriend, damn it!'

'Whatever she is, I'm still nervous,' she retorted. 'I've no idea what's really expected of me, and I know that when I make an almighty hash of whatever it is you're going to think I've done so deliberately! That's all I was trying to say.'

'I made it perfectly plain what is expected of you, and there's absolutely no reason why you should make a hash of it, as long as you do as you're told,' he informed her coldly. 'But if you do, you're damned right—I *shall* assume it was deliberate.'

'You made *nothing* in the least plain,' she retorted angrily. 'And don't for one moment think I'm stupid enough to believe that ridiculous story you concocted, because——'

'Lindy, I don't give a toss what you believe,' he cut in icily. 'Just don't contemplate playing silly games, because you'll most certainly regret it.'

'And don't you dare threaten me!' she exploded. 'I've no idea what sort of convoluted game it is *you're* playing with this Arista, nor what it is you have to lose if it goes wrong. But, much as I'd love to see you get whatever come-uppance may be due to you on that score, Niko, I've no intention of jeopardising the freedom you've so magnanimously agreed to give me for the sake of witnessing it—of that you can be certain!'

'I didn't ask you to pay back your wretched husband's debts in the first place,' he drawled. 'I am right, am I not, in assuming that's the freedom to which you so scathingly refer?'

'Yes . . . that and my being allowed to leave here,' muttered Lindy, suddenly not in the least sure that her leaving had actually been part of the agreement.

'Now you're trying to change the rules as you go along,' he murmured, then smiled across at her with dazzling insincerity. 'That's not to say I'm ruling out their being reviewed, should Arista's visit go without a hitch.' He rose, that same insincere smile firmly in place as he sauntered over to her. 'Though you have to bear in mind—as I've already pointed out to you—that my gaining possession of you was a matter quite apart from those other follies of your husband's.' He gazed down at her, frowning as his eyes flickered critically over her. 'Stand up,' he muttered.

'Now what?' groaned Lindy, wondering just how much more of this she could take as she glared up at him, while a pleading voice of sanity urgently reminded her that at least he had agreed to consider letting her leave after all this was over.

'Lindy, just stand up, will you?'

Her lips clamping into an angry line, she got to her feet.

'Now, that wasn't so terribly difficult, was it?' he murmured, his hands reaching out to tug free the ribbon tying up her hair. 'That pony-tailed-*ingénue* look hardly goes with what you're wearing,' he observed drily, his fingers raking through her hair and fluffing it to fullness around her face.

'Have you ever considered taking up hairdressing?' snapped Lindy, furiously trying to twist free from those trespassing fingers and the unnerving effect they were already beginning to have. 'If not, you should—you'd probably do well at it!'

He laughed. 'I didn't for one second believe you'd actually be capable of grovelling,' he mocked, yanking her sharply against him. 'But I suggest you start practising a suitably dewy-eyed look—our guest will be here soon.'

Lindy instantly lowered her eyes to the front of his shirt and clamped her arms tightly to her sides. This time, no matter what he tried, she would resist him, she vowed frantically; even if it meant holding her breath and suffocating herself in the process!

'Oh, dear, Lindy, don't tell me you can't even muster the glimmer of a dewy-eyed look for me,' he sighed, his head lowering till his lips were brushing against her temple. 'After all, I'm not nearly as grotesque as I was—I hardly limp at all now, and you have to admit that hideously disfiguring scar on my head has faded even more than the one on my leg. So——'

'Stop it! Niko, I'm just not in the mood for this,' pleaded Lindy through clenched teeth.

'Not in the mood for romance?' he gasped, as though unable to believe his ears.

'Niko, you're about as romantic as a ... as a——'

'Lindy, I'm the most romantic of men,' he protested, laughter growling softly in his throat as his lips began dropping feather-light kisses against her temple. 'The most incredibly romantic of men,' he whispered dreamily while his mouth began working its way down and across her cheek, lingering teasingly as it reached the tip of her nose and then moving on. By the time he had criss-crossed her entire face, diligently avoiding her lips, her fingernails had begun slicing into her palms from the strain of preventing herself from reacting.

'Come on, Lindy, loosen up,' he coaxed, his mouth suddenly against hers; not kissing it, barely even touching it as his lips brushed back and forth hypnotically against hers. 'Put your arms around me,' he pleaded, his lips still a tantalising whisper on hers.

'Let me go,' protested Lindy. 'I've absolutely no wish to put my arms around you.'

The force with which she uttered that lie had the unfortunate effect of bringing her lips into an inordinate amount of contact with his—a fact that wrought only more havoc on her already seriously impaired senses.

'Liar—you're scared of putting your arms around me,' he teased huskily.

'Why on earth should I be scared?' she demanded recklessly.

'I've no idea—but you can only prove you're not by doing so,' he whispered, a new note of urgency entering his voice.

It occurred to her that there might have seemed a strong element of indecent haste in the speed with which her arms had risen to cling around his neck—an impression she swiftly sought to redress.

'There—I've done it.' The coolly dismissive words, intended to put him firmly in his place and restore some sorely needed faith in her own will-power, staggered from her lips in a softly inviting whisper.

'Lindy, I . . . Oh, hell!' he groaned, his arms suddenly crushing her to him as his mouth began devouring hers with a hungry intensity.

She had been unable to keep the rash vow she had made to herself only moments before, but he certainly hadn't meant this to happen, a small voice sang out inside her as her body burst to trembling life in reflex response to the ardent heat of his... Niko was no longer in total control of himself.

Yet as her lips reciprocated the searing passion of his, and even as her body melted to mould in open acquiescence to the uninhibitedly virile sensuality of his, there was a part of her that shrank in fear from the alien yearnings threatening to overpower her.

Then there was no part of her that wasn't entirely awash with the stinging sweetness of the excitement surging through her as his hands roved her body in questing impatience.

'I suppose the intelligent thing to do would be to move you into my room as of now,' he groaned softly, burying his face against the creamy curve of her throat. 'Don't you agree?'

There had been sufficient hint of a barb in that final question to bring his previous words into sharp focus in the still heady confusion of her mind. And almost as she made to draw free from the sense-sapping sanctuary of his arms, so he had already raised his head and drawn back from her.

'I've already told you how I abhor sexual coyness in a woman,' he reminded her with devastating candour, the heat of passion clearing from his eyes with a speed that jarred her harshly back to her senses, 'and neither of us has been under any illusions as to where this would lead.'

'Is that so?' managed Lindy, her every muscle so painfully tensed that she was amazed to find her jaw had been capable of producing those stalling words.

'Yes—it's so,' he replied implacably. 'But not only that: it would make it so much easier for me to resist the delectable Arista's wiles were I to have you to pre-occupy and distract me.'

It was only when the open palm of her hand made stinging contact with the side of his face that Lindy became aware of what she was doing, and in the same instant a sharp cry of pain exploded from her as her hand was caught and her arm twisted agonisingly behind her.

'Not only was that a very foolish thing to do, but it was also very dangerous,' he rasped, his voice hoarse with rage. 'You're not an inexperienced girl being clumsily propositioned by a callow youth—you're an experienced, not to mention married woman who should know better than to resort to violence simply because she doesn't like having the truth spelled out to her!' He released her arm with a dismissive gesture of contempt. 'And don't ever make the mistake of hitting me again, because I might then be tempted to demonstrate how easily violence can be overcome by violence.'

Rubbing distractedly at a shoulder she felt sure had been close to being dislocated, she felt tempted to inform him that he had already proved his point. It was a temptation she resisted with considerable difficulty as she glared up into the cold contempt of his eyes.

'As you're so fond of dishing out the truth to others, perhaps you won't object to receiving some,' she informed him, gathering up the few remnants left of her pride and clinging to them for dear life. 'Unlike you, I don't hold the view that a vague sexual attraction leads automatically to leaping into bed and satisfying it.' She was giving herself a mental pat on the back for the cool succinctness of her statement when his drawling interruption scattered her self-congratulatory thoughts.

'Vague? My dear Lindy, my mind positively boggles at the thought of how you might respond were you to feel positive sexual attraction.'

Rattled to have had the flaw in her statement so promptly pointed out to her, she launched straight back into attack.

'And, for one who is so fond of pontificating to others, I'm amazed you had the gall to bring up my marital status. I'd have thought the last thing a self-professed paragon of virtue such as yourself would stoop to is an affair with a married woman!'

She felt something close to elation as the words were spilling from her—it was only when they were finished that she began experiencing the odd twinge of doubt. It was the disconcertingly inscrutable look he gave her, before moving over to one of the chairs and sitting himself down, that heightened those unspecified doubts.

'Ah...your marriage,' he murmured, savouring each word. 'I was beginning to wonder when, if ever, you intended getting around to that interesting little topic.'

Lindy took a reflex step back and found herself up against the edge of the sofa. She promptly sat down.

'You know, most of the time I find myself forgetting that you are a married woman...a memory lapse we seem to share.' He leaned back in his chair with an air of complete relaxation. 'But, to return to what you were saying, I doubt if I have ever been described as a paragon of virtue, and I most certainly could never make any claims to being one,' he murmured with conversational ease. 'But you're right in that I would instinctively regard any married woman as taboo. Morally, culturally and in any other way that could be mentioned I would regard an affair with another man's wife as totally unacceptable.'

Though she was the one who had posed the question, and even though she could see that his answer must surely be to her advantage, Lindy found herself at a complete loss for words. It was something he had an infuriating knack of doing, she told herself frustratedly, reducing her to gibbering fury with his outrageous utterances one moment, then in the next stunning her to silence with words and sentiments that could well have been her own!

'But I suppose there's always the exception... and it seems as though you're the exception to this particular rule of mine.'

'Well, *my* rules don't happen to have exceptions!' she exploded with reckless vehemence. 'It takes two to tango... and I have no intention of tangoing with you!'

Even halfway through those words, she was frantically trying to stop them, and by the time they had burst their way from her she was too mortified by them even to resent the soft laughter they had brought bubbling from him.

'Well, I suppose that if you're given to euphemisms that's as good as any,' he chuckled, reaching towards the telephone as it started ringing beside him.

Her cheeks scarlet with humiliation, Lindy scrabbled to get a grip on herself as he muttered a few words into the receiver, rising to his feet as he replaced it.

'How nice—our guest has arrived,' he murmured.

Lindy's heart and stomach met as each lurched in opposite directions.

'What am I supposed to do?' she croaked, her words a genuine plea for specific guidance.

'Nothing,' he retorted, striding past her and towards the door.

'Niko... I meant what I said... I honestly am very nervous!'

'There's nothing to be nervous about. You can occupy yourself with practising that dewy-eyed look I mentioned while I get Arista settled in.' He opened the door and was halfway through it before he paused and called back to her. 'You could also give some thought to the one failing I have that I can't deny—that of resorting to anything to get what I really want...even learning to tango.'

CHAPTER SEVEN

THE first time Lindy had seen Niko Leandros she had recognised in him the embodiment of all she, and no doubt countless other women, regarded as physical perfection in a man ... it had been no more than a recognition of fact, because Niko Leandros was simply a devastatingly handsome man.

The thought that had struck her on meeting Arista Tatalias had been that in this svelte, ebony-haired and slightly taller than average woman she was seeing what countless men would no doubt regard as the female equivalent of Niko Leandros ... because Arista Tatalias was simply quite breathtakingly beautiful.

And Arista was Niko's female equivalent in other less appealing ways, thought Lindy grimly, trying to stop herself from glaring across the lunch table at the woman preoccupying her disgruntled thoughts—especially in the dismissive arrogance with which she tended to look down that perfectly structured nose of hers at other less fortunate mortals; in this case, the waiter to whom she was issuing instructions in that low, perpetually husky-sounding voice of hers. In fact, Lindy decided, she had never met a less friendly, more snooty woman than the gorgeous-looking Arista.

'I've told them to wait a while before serving lunch,' Arista informed her, consulting her companion having been a consideration that obviously wouldn't have occurred to her. 'I presume Niko intends turning up—where is he?'

110

Lindy managed to suppress a look of surprise. She hadn't seen Niko all morning, but had assumed he was with Arista—just as she had assumed he had been with the woman all those other times during which he had disappeared in the past couple of days.

'He's been rather busy lately,' stated Lindy, torn between countermanding Arista's cavalier delaying of lunch and a positive dread of spending an entire meal alone in her company—the meals the three of them had shared had been ordeal enough for her as it was!

'Busy?' queried Arista coolly. 'Niko's not interested in this anachronism of a place—he's closing it down.'

'Which is probably why he's so busy,' replied Lindy evenly, determined not to allow herself to become rattled by that faintly patronising tone. 'I should think there's rather a lot to be done—winding down a business of this size.' And that, she suddenly realised, most probably did account for Niko's long disappearances—even before the arrival of this unwanted guest.

'A business of this size?' chortled Arista. 'My dear, have you any idea of the size of the Leandros Corporation? A chain of hotels like this would be peanuts by comparison!'

Lindy masked her growing irritation behind a dismissive shrug. Any feelings of sympathy she had had towards this woman had been dispelled almost the instant she had met her. She couldn't remember a single exchange they had had which had not contained one barely veiled barb or another.

'Perhaps winding down a small business needs more concentrated attention than running a very large one,' she muttered, and immediately wished she hadn't when it struck her how gauche she must have sounded.

'You're probably right,' Arista confused her by saying: and confused her even further by suddenly smiling brightly and signalling for one of the waiters. 'Let's order our lunch now—it's about time we had the chance to have a chat on our own.'

While Arista gave her attention to the waiter, Lindy gave hers to collecting her wits. As far as she was concerned, a chat on their own was what both of them had been avoiding like the plague.

'I'm sure you can understand how guilty I've been feeling about everything,' sighed Arista. 'But I had to come here to make sure Niko was all right—and he is, isn't he, Lindy?'

Alarm bells had begun jangling nervously in Lindy's head. She had no knowledge whatever of what it was she was expected to understand Arista's guilt over, and she had a horrible feeling that she was about to be subjected to what could amount to the third degree by a woman she could bring herself neither to like nor trust.

'I'm sure you can see for yourself how much better he is,' she replied cagily. 'And he hardly even limps now.'

'But can you imagine what it was like at the time?' exclaimed Arista heatedly. 'When they said they would probably have to remove his leg... something terrible happened inside me!'

Lindy's eyes widened in horror—it had never occurred to her that his injury had been quite that severe, even though he had been as unforthcoming with details of his accident as he had with Arista's visit. But now she was conscious of a driving need within her to protect him from her own ignorance, despite the fact that it was an ignorance brought about solely by his infuriating reticence, and she recognised it as a need apart from anything she could hope to gain in the process.

'Niko doesn't discuss his accident,' she stated quietly, accepting that she had no option but to be honest on that score at least.

'No—I suppose he wouldn't.'

Again Lindy found herself thrown by Arista's reply, and was conscious of the woman's eyes never once leaving her as the return of the waiters brought a silence between them.

'Surely you can see that he's only using you to punish me!' exclaimed Arista the instant the waiters were out of earshot.

'Why should Niko want to punish you?' asked Lindy, forcing her unwilling attention to the food before her as a strange mixture of emotions began assailing her.

'When you say that Niko doesn't discuss his accident with you, does that include his not having told you that I was his passenger when it happened?' demanded Arista, her flashing eyes now almost as black as the dramatic cloud of her hair curling exotically to her shoulders.

Lindy nodded. 'I know very little—hardly anything— about the accident.'

Arista's dark eyes widened with a gleam that was curiously like satisfaction. 'It's a wonder we weren't both killed—and all because of some wretched child running out in front of us.'

Lindy felt herself shiver as something in those words told her that had Arista been at the wheel the child wouldn't have stood a chance.

'Niko's beautiful car was a complete write-off,' continued the Greek woman, her tone conveying far more concern over the car than it had over the child. 'And naturally he was frantic with worry about me—I was barely conscious. Of course, I didn't learn until much later that it was in his desperation to rescue me that he did so much further damage to his crushed leg.'

Lindy's imagination was working overtime, and she wasn't enjoying the pictures it was so vividly portraying one little bit—yet Niko's damaged leg barely featured in them.

'Well ... as I said, he's barely limping now,' she muttered, racking her brains for something to say that could change the subject.

'You still don't understand, do you?' said Arista, her eyes fixing Lindy's across the table with barely concealed contempt. 'I was badly shaken up by the accident—though, mercifully, I got away with no more than slight concussion and bad bruising. But when I heard they were thinking of amputating Niko's leg...' She broke off to give a theatrical shudder of horror. 'I still don't know what it was that got into me, but, no matter how much the poor darling begged to see me, I simply couldn't face him. Even on the fifth day, when I was discharged, I couldn't bring myself to go and say goodbye to him.'

Lindy felt her fingers tightening round her fork and had to make a conscious effort to stop herself smashing it down against the plate. She could so easily understand now why Niko had been so reluctant to come out with the truth—his pride wouldn't let him! And he *was* using her to inflict retributive punishment on Arista—for deserting him when he had most needed her. One thing she now realised was that Niko and Arista were two of a kind and that they thoroughly deserved each other.

'And that's why, to be perfectly candid, I want him back...'

Suddenly aware that she had probably been being spoken to for some time, Lindy glanced over at the woman glowering challengingly at her across the table and was thankful to feel her own face freeze to expressionlessness.

'...and why I'll do anything in my power to ensure I get him back,' Arista was finishing.

Lindy was tempted to retort 'you're welcome', biting back the words just in time as she remembered how much she stood to lose should she give in to her anger and disgust. Instead she gave a non-committal shrug, then turned her attention pointedly to her meal.

When she had finished she stood up. 'Do excuse me; I'm going for a swim.' And she was, she told herself as she rose and left the room. It might be the worst thing she could do after a meal, but right now she craved the cooling cleansing of water more than she had ever craved anything in her life.

This time there had been no solace to be had in the water, she accepted bitterly as she made her way back to the suite, her heart filled with a leaden heaviness.

'Mrs Russell.'

She turned, finding irony in the shudder of protest that still shot through her in response to that form of address.

'Maria,' she murmured, smiling. Like the rest of the skeleton staff now manning the hotel, the gentle dark-haired receptionist would soon be gone. As she knew had been the case with the vast majority of the staff, Maria had known no other job than her one here, and with it went her accommodation. The thought of what was to happen to the girl, and to all of the staff, troubled Lindy deeply.

'I forgot to tell Mr Niko that his mother rang from New York—she wants him to ring her back.'

'I'll tell him when I see him,' promised Lindy, her smile dying to a look of hopeless dejection as the lift doors closed behind her.

The first thing she heard, as she began opening the door to the suite, was the rumbling deepness of Niko's voice. But it was the husky softness of Arista's laughter that choked the breath in her lungs with a constricting, painful tightness even before she had opened the door sufficiently to witness their bodies silhouetted as one against the bright backdrop of light-reflecting glass.

As though she was unaware of any intrusion, Arista's head remained tilted back as she leaned back in Niko's arms, her hands resting lightly against his chest while she laughed up at him.

It was Niko's head which turned towards Lindy, standing frozen in the doorway; but it was only his head that moved, his arms remaining around the slim body of the woman held in them.

'I...there's a message for you,' she stammered in shock and was appalled to hear in her words a note of the chaos churning wildly within her mind.

'Is that so?' murmured Niko, his tone almost amused as his arms released Arista. 'I do hope you haven't leapt to any wrong conclusions over this little scene,' he added in that same tone of amusement as he removed Arista's hands from his chest. 'Now tell me, what was the message?'

'Your mother rang from New York—she wants you to ring her.'

Almost before she had finished uttering those words Arista had broken into a rushed spate in Greek, her voice rising in protest.

Niko's features tightened to instant harshness as, in the same language, he cut into that agitated rush of words.

With a strange feeling of disembodiment, Lindy watched the scene before her. The only thing she had to go on was the tone of the words being spoken and she knew the moment Arista had won him over in whatever it was they were arguing about; and she knew it even before he leaned forward with a soft chuckle and silenced the husky protests of the woman in his arms with a teasing kiss on her pouting lips.

'It's very rude of us to speak Greek like this in front of Lindy,' he admonished, turning from Arista and making his way towards Lindy. 'I'm sure she must be feeling very neglected, our damp little water-sprite.'

Lindy watched his progress towards her as though seeing his movements in slow motion. And she could hear a voice shrieking out within her to do something—say something—before she made a complete fool of herself; but she found herself unable to respond to that voice in the slightest.

'Lindy?'

It was only when he reached out and prised her fingers from around the heavy brass doorknob that she became conscious of the fierceness of her grip on it. And it was only when she felt his arm descend across her shoulders and felt his fingers tap lightly against her arm, as though summoning her back to wakefulness, that her senses began staggering back into synchronisation.

'Any other messages for me?' he asked, the pressure of his fingers increasing with warning impatience.

'None as contentious as that last, I hope,' murmured Arista, joining them at the door. She glanced up at Niko, challenge a caress in her eyes. 'I suppose I might as well get some packing done—as I'll be leaving rather early in the morning.'

'I suppose you might as well,' agreed Niko, his lips quirking in amusement.

Having given Lindy the briefest of nods, Arista then reached up and kissed Niko on the cheek, the waft of her scent lingering in the air as the door closed behind her.

'I wasn't in the least sure how I was supposed to react to that tender little scene,' muttered Lindy, still having

problems dragging both her mind and body out of the
stupefying torpor in which they had become locked. She
slipped free of his arm, and it took her conscious effort
not to run as she made her way across the room. She
drew open one of the huge plate-glass doors, desperate
for a breath of the cool, fresh air that would clear her
nostrils of the scent clinging to them with cloying
pervasiveness.

'You reacted well—just the right degree of stunned
disbelief,' he stated, the hint of wariness in his words,
as he joined her by the open door, sending a shiver of
foreboding through her as she waited for him to continue. 'Though I must say, for a moment you had me
worried that you were about to overdo it...swoon,
perhaps—or create a scene of jealous outrage.' He
laughed, then gave a sudden shiver. 'Do we really have
to have that howling wind blowing in like that?'

Lindy closed the door in silence, not trusting herself
to take his words at their face value. Arista—the woman
he found so desirable, the woman he wanted to punish
for deserting him when he most needed her—wanted him
back...and was well on her way to getting him back,
she thought bitterly, judging by what she had just
witnessed.

Jealousy was a problem she had never had to contend
with, but she felt sure her pride would prevent her cre-
ating a scene, should that problem ever arise. And as
for swooning—she simply wasn't the type! But, as far
as she knew, a spinning head, legs threatening to buckle
and the mind going numbingly blank were some of the
symptoms associated with swooning...all of which she
had just experienced in those nightmarish few moments.

'Who gave you the message about my mother's having
rung?' he asked, moving away to fling himself down on
one of the armchairs.

'Maria,' replied Lindy, frowning as she realised it seemed to have been that message that had triggered off the exchange between himself and Arista.

'Are you happy to hear that Arista will be leaving in the morning?' he enquired in his customary taunting manner.

Lindy felt first a flash of anger at his tone, then puzzlement... she had been so preoccupied that the fact that Arista was leaving hadn't really sunk in.

'It's immaterial to me whether she goes or stays,' she lied. 'I'd have thought you'd be the one to be happy to hear she's leaving.'

'You feel you know me well enough to judge what will or will not make me happy, do you, Lindy?' he drawled, his mocking gaze accompanying her as she walked to the sofa and sat down.

'I was merely drawing conclusions from the claims you yourself made,' she retorted coldly. 'I neither know nor care what makes you happy or otherwise.' Why couldn't he be civil just for once?

'I see,' he murmured. 'Well, one thing that doesn't make me in the least happy is to hear that my mother's on to me here,' he startled her by adding.

Her surprise showed in the look she flashed him, though she was now remembering Arista's remark that the message had been contentious.

He shrugged as he gave a grim laugh. 'I didn't wish my parents to know anything about my accident until I'd been signed off once and for all by my doctors.'

'How on earth could you manage to keep such a thing from your own parents?' she exclaimed—and why would he want to?

With a flash of impatience he answered both those questions. 'Fairly easily—or so I'd thought, as they live most of the time in New York. They'd only just returned to the States after my great-uncle's death and I really didn't see any point in burdening them with more bad news.'

The fact that he could be so caring towards his parents didn't alter the fact that he could also be a callous monster, Lindy reminded herself angrily, but despite that reminder there was a softening in her that was reflected in her next words to him.

'Niko, I'm sure your doctors will sign you off very soon—you seem incredibly fit to me.'

The sceptical look with which he met those words killed any softness stone-dead in her.

'What a comfort it is to hear you say that,' he drawled. 'Perhaps you'll come along when I'm next examined—and give the medical team the benefit of your expert opinion.'

'Have you any friends, Niko?' she asked, shaking with fury. 'Because I'd be most surprised to hear you had!'

'Are you trying to tell me your assessment of my fitness was merely a friendly overture?' he enquired.

'Oh, for heaven's sake!' exclaimed Lindy in angry exasperation. 'I apologise for having had the temerity to remark on your apparent state of health without having any medical knowledge with which to back it up—satisfied?'

'If your aim is to satisfy me you certainly won't achieve it by trying to be friendly,' he murmured, insolent challenge in his look. 'In fact, your friendship doesn't interest me in the least—it's your body I want.'

For one stunned moment Lindy found herself trying to rationalise her way out of believing she had heard what she most certainly had heard. No man in his right mind—no matter how rude and argumentative, no matter how arrogantly careless of the feelings of others—could sit in such complete relaxation, halfway across a room from a woman, and come out with a remark like that...and in tones so matter-of-fact! No man, that was, except one as callous and egotistical as Niko Leandros!

Without uttering a single word, she rose and left.

In her room she stripped from her swimming things and, shunning the clothes that were part of a lifestyle to which she was a total stranger, dressed herself instead in the comforting familiarity of her jeans and an old Guernsey sweater she had once borrowed from her father and had never got around to returning.

She dried her hair and tied it back in a pony-tail, doggedly trying to strip her mind from its sudden and vivid reliving of the sensation of Niko's fingers in her hair as he had loosened it from this same style.

As she left the suite she sensed rather than saw him still seated as he had been, his body as ever maintaining its sartorial elegance even as it sprawled in complete relaxation.

As she reached the shore she turned and glanced up towards the hotel, her steps quickening as she saw his tall figure now on the balcony, gazing down at her.

She walked the few hundred yards that was the beach-line, then clambered over spray-slicked rocks until she could go no further. Then she sat down on one of the rocks, gazing out to sea while the demons, so long skulking in the recesses of her mind, finally began their rampage. It wasn't simply that she was homesick and eaten up with a loneliness such as she had never before experienced, those demons taunted her. There was fear lurking beneath the loneliness and confusion she had discovered on this lovely, isolated island; a fear of those stirrings within her of her true, hitherto unacknowledged, self and of the passions that simmered within her, impatient for release. And then there was jealousy, taunted those merciless demons; her first taste of which had so devastated her that it festered on within her, demanding the attention she still couldn't bring herself to give to it. And love?

Shaking her head in vehement denial, she leapt to her feet, her gaze rising involuntarily to where that tall figure still stood immobile on the balcony.

He was using her, she reminded herself savagely as a fatal softness began laying siege to her. He was using her to avenge himself on the woman who had let him down so badly, yet against whose attraction he still couldn't trust himself.

Her steps faltered as she fought off the voice inside her reminding her of those glimpses she had had of the true Niko; the man who, despite his disclaimers, had been moved by her tears; who had protected his parents at a time when even the most hardened sophisticate might have called on their support; the man whose views on love and marriage so exactly mirrored her own; the man who, whatever his true feelings for Arista, found himself physically attracted to a woman he believed to be married—and who hated both himself and her because of that attraction. And who could blame him? In his eyes she was a woman who had exchanged marriage vows for the most spurious of reasons and who now treated those vows with the contempt with which she had apparently entered into them. The man she claimed to be married to was a scoundrel and, for all Niko knew, she had been a willing accomplice who had, in the end, been abandoned. And she had judged him—had resented the open contempt with which he regarded her, she accused herself bitterly…how else could she possibly expect him to regard her?

'I must say, Vasilis really is the most excellent chef!' exclaimed Arista at the end of their unquestionably superb meal. 'What's going to happen to him now that you've decided to close down the hotel?'

Lindy's ears pricked. Yes, she wanted to expand, what was to happen to all the staff—most of whom had been with the hotel for their entire working lives?

'He tells me he's retiring—but I'll believe that only when I see it,' replied Niko with a chuckle. 'He's bought a restaurant in Athens, which his two sons run.'

'My, you must be giving him a more than generous severance pay,' murmured Arista, draining her wine glass and immediately refilling it—as she had done several times throughout the meal.

Though frowning as he watched her, Niko gave another chuckle. 'All the staff deserve every penny of what I'm giving them—though every single one of them will justifiably regard it as peanuts.'

'Justifiably?' snorted Arista. 'I'd say that was most ungrateful of them!'

'It's justifiable because, by comparison to what they're all worth—in hard cash—it *is* peanuts,' he admonished. 'You see, my uncle left them all extremely well provided-for in his will.'

'All of them?' exclaimed Arista, aghast, as Lindy gave a silent cheer.

'Every single one.'

Arista chuckled and rolled her eyes in mock surprise. 'My, that uncle of yours really must have been an eccentric!' she said, draining her glass and signalling for a waiter when she discovered the wine bottle to be empty.

'He did what any decent individual who could afford it would have done, and they deserve every penny of what they got,' stated Niko sharply, intercepting the waiter as he arrived and speaking quietly to him in Greek. 'I'm having coffee sent up to the suite.'

'And some more wine?' pouted Arista as he got to his feet.

He muttered something to her, again in Greek.

'Spoil-sport,' she laughed, raising her arms above her head and stretching with the luxuriating lithesomeness of a cat as she gazed flirtatiously up at him.

Lindy leapt to her feet, a hot wave of pure jealousy shooting through her as Niko helped Arista to her feet with a mutter that was more amused than exasperated.

'Oh, dear, perhaps you're right, darling,' said Arista, chuckling huskily as she snuggled against Niko in the lift. 'Perhaps I have had just the tiniest bit too much to drink.'

'There's no perhaps about it,' he laughed, his eyes soft as they gazed down at the luxuriant profusion of dark hair spilled across the paleness of his jacket. 'Thank God the coffee's arrived,' he added as they stepped from the lift to find a waiter holding the door open for them, 'because you need some.' He grinned at Arista as he removed her from him.

Arista turned to Lindy, her smile stunning. 'Why don't you pour the coffee while I get some music on?' she suggested, breezing into the suite and across the room with a sudden sureness that made Lindy suspect that the amount she had drunk had had little effect on her. 'Niko, I really do think it's about time you got back into the social scene again—it's no fun without you!'

Suddenly the room was filled with music. Lindy glanced over to where Arista was standing by one of the wood-fronted recesses, now opened—she hadn't even realised there was any hi-fi equipment there... and certainly not equipment this powerful, she thought, wincing as the volume increased deafeningly.

She lowered her head and began pouring the coffee as Niko roared out in Greek—obviously for the sound to be turned down, she decided as the volume subsided a fraction.

'Come and dance, Niko,' pleaded Arista, twirling around on her own.

'I don't want to dance,' he muttered, picking up a cup and walking to the balcony doors, where he stood gazing out into the darkness.

'Heavens, you've turned into a real killjoy, darling,' complained Arista. 'What have you done to him?' she called to Lindy. 'He used to be such fun! Lindy, tell him he's got to dance with me!'

Lindy busied herself by taking a drink from her cup. She wasn't in the least fooled by this tipsy act of Arista's and she didn't intend letting herself be used as a pawn in whatever it was the woman was plotting.

'Lindy!'

'Arista, he's already told you he doesn't want to,' snapped Lindy. 'Perhaps his leg isn't up to it.'

'*He* has two legs, both of which are functioning normally,' growled Niko, his back still to the room. 'And, if I remember rightly, I was diagnosed as being incredibly fit today.'

Thrown by the venom in his tone, Lindy watched in stunned silence as he walked to an alcove, placed his cup on one of the shelves and then turned to Arista.

'You're right,' he murmured, opening his arms to her. 'Perhaps I should start thinking about getting back into the swing of things.'

As she stepped into his arms Arista murmured something to him in Greek, and it was his softly chuckled reply in the same language that brought Lindy a sudden and overwhelming feeling of isolation.

For a while she almost succeeded in fooling herself into believing that she could remain unaffected by what was taking place before her, forcing her eyes to follow them as they danced, only to find them dropping in anguish seconds later to the hands clenched tightly in her lap. And, though her eyes remained lowered, they still carried a vivid picture of two bodies, swaying as though one in rhythmic perfection.

It was the sound of their voices, exchanging softly whispered words of which she could never be a part, that once again lifted Lindy's gaze to them. His face cupped in Arista's hands, Niko was laughing down into her upturned face, and as his arms moved lazily against that slim body and his head lowered Lindy rose and left the room, certain in the knowledge that her leaving would make no more impression on them than had her presence.

CHAPTER EIGHT

LINDY awoke to a distant ringing sound, an uncomfortable heaviness weighing down her body as she sat up in bed.

For several seconds she gazed uncertainly around her while her mind struggled to free itself from the dark grip of its dreams. Except that she hadn't been dreaming, she realised numbly as the memories returned: it had been a nightmare... but she hadn't been dreaming.

She shook her head, trying to clear it of that still persisting ringing sound, then realised it was the telephone she was hearing.

She heaved herself from the bed, that almost drugged feeling of heaviness remaining with her as she stumbled down the marbled corridors.

'Hello? Oh, Maria! I don't think Mr Niko is here.'

'No—he had to go to the hospital. There's——'

'Hospital?' exclaimed Lindy, a terrible feeling of panic shooting through her.

'Today is another of his check-up days,' explained the receptionist, her matter-of-fact tone instantly assuaging Lindy's panic. 'Mrs Russell, I rang to tell you there's a call for you.'

'For me?' echoed Lindy, wishing her head would clear.

'From Mr Russell.'

'From Tim?' she groaned disbelievingly. 'I...' She broke off, struggling to get a grip on herself. 'Thanks, Maria, put it through, will you, please?'

'Hello, Lindy! How are things?'

There really was something wrong with the way her mind was functioning, thought Lindy dazedly as Tim Russell's cheerily unconcerned words blasted against her ear.

'How would you expect things to be?' she demanded angrily once she had managed to get a grip on herself. 'Tim, I can hardly believe——'

'Lindy, I behaved like an absolute rat,' cut in Tim, 'and I can't blame you for wanting to blow your top, but don't—I've good news!'

'What—that the police have caught up with you?' demanded Lindy bitterly.

'Lindy, I know what you must be thinking of me, but I intend making up for that. I've come into quite a bit of money and——'

'Who did you steal it from this time?'

'Lindy, I swear to God, I'd never done anything like that before—thieving just isn't part of my normal nature. I know I wasn't honest about how I felt about you, but I wanted you—I actually wanted to marry you, damn it!'

'And what about this other woman you were supposed to be broken-hearted over?' she demanded and immediately could have kicked herself for having bothered to bring it up.

'I was—until I fell for you!' he protested. 'But, let's face it, Lindy, the way you were feeling about men when I appeared on the scene you'd have run a mile if I'd been honest. Just you wait till you fall in love yourself and it all goes wrong…it can change your whole personality!'

Lindy's knuckles whitened from the intensity with which she was gripping the receiver. Apart from the fact that the sort of facile emotion he was referring to could hardly be described as love, perhaps he had a point, she admitted bitterly, but she wasn't planning anything like a robbery... at least, not yet!

'Lindy, the amount I'm sending is a large one—enough to cover *all* my debts. You see, apart from what I took from Leandros, there are these three other people——'

'I know all about them,' Lindy interrupted him sharply. 'Niko settled all your debts with them.'

'Niko?' murmured Tim archly. 'Perhaps I didn't do you such a bad turn after all.'

'Oh, no?' rasped Lindy, shaking with anger. 'For what you did to me you'd be well advised never to cross my path again!'

'Oh, dear,' he muttered. 'And to think I took you for a girl who was more than capable of looking after herself, if you know what I mean,' he added with the callous lack of concern of a man most definitely not in love with her.

'I know *exactly* what you mean, and you can rest assured that you were right,' she replied scathingly. 'But you'd still be safer staying clear of my path!'

'Anyway, about this bank draft,' he said. 'The extra is for you—to cover the salary I owe you and what I borrowed from you—plus your fare back to London.'

'And how am I supposed to get back to London without a passport?' she demanded coldly.

'Try asking Leandros for it back,' retorted Tim. 'I'd have thought he'd be glad to see the back of you by now—especially as he's not getting what he obviously hoped for from you.'

'You really make me sick!' exploded Lindy. 'And I'll never forgive you for what you've done to me—not for as long as I live!'

She flung down the receiver, then leaned wearily against the wall, battling against the threat of tears.

'*Just you wait till you fall in love yourself and it all goes wrong... it can change your whole personality*!'

The fact that she had sobbed herself to sleep last night had been personality change enough for her, she informed herself savagely, her shoulders squaring determinedly as she straightened and marched back to her room.

By the time she had showered and dressed she was feeling almost calm. Once the money arrived she would be able to pay Niko what he was owed and leave, she told herself, frowning as doubt began rippling across her fragile calm. Tim was right—he probably would be glad to see the back of her, she reasoned, then immediately found herself wondering how often she had known Niko react in any way that was predictable. But once those debts were cleared she was leaving whether he liked it or not, she vowed—what say had he in the matter anyway?

Fuming away to herself, she left the suite and made her way to Reception. Just because he seemed to regard himself as some sort of feudal lord here didn't mean to say she had to go along with it! It was her passport, for heaven's sake, and he had no right to it!

Feeling almost like a criminal, she entered the office and took the keys of the safe from one of the drawers.

The chance that Niko had returned her passport to the safe was negligible, she told herself as she inserted the keys in the door with trembling hands, but one she had to check before she really started her search.

The sickening ferocity with which her heart plummeted as she re-closed the door surprised her—she had been virtually certain she wouldn't find her passport there anyway.

But she had to find it—she would go out of her mind if she didn't get away from here soon, she warned herself frantically. And though she knew where it was she should make her search, she headed off in exactly the opposite direction, out of the hotel and down through the grounds, along paths she had explored in her first days here.

She kept on walking until at last enough of the confusion had calmed from her mind to lead her back to the inevitable issue of her passport. Only once she had it in her possession could she start indulging in the luxury of making plans for her escape. She turned to retrace her steps and spent her entire journey back wrestling with the problem of how she was actually going to bring herself to do what she knew she had to.

By early evening, her scruples about what she was doing ruthlessly suppressed, she systematically searched every nook and cranny in the suite—bar one room.

Close to tears of frustration, she then stood outside that one room, steeling herself to go in and search it, as she had always known in her heart of hearts she would have to.

The only place it could be was in Niko's room, she argued angrily with herself...which was why, if she really wanted her passport so desperately, she should have searched there in the first place! So what was she frightened of? she demanded scathingly of herself. If Arista had spent the night with him it was hardly likely to be blazoned across the walls in neon lights! Or did she simply want an excuse to remain trapped here and to go slowly out of her mind?

Her face grim with determination, she opened the door and marched into the room. It was larger than the one she occupied and starkly masculine in its noticeable lack of decorative embellishments, she noticed before she pulled herself up sharply with a reminder of the task in hand.

Her hands shaking and her heart thudding painfully against her ribs, she began searching through the tall chest of drawers nearest her. Her heart far from in it, she found herself opening one drawer after another, slamming each shut with barely a glance at its contents. And all the while she could feel the breath caught suffocatingly in her throat.

This was crazy, she told herself dementedly, pushing closed the last of the drawers. She simply wasn't capable of this prying into another person's things...she couldn't go through with it!

Calmed by her decision not to continue, she turned to leave, and froze as a carved writing bureau in the corner of the room caught her eye. Taking a deep breath, she forced her reluctant legs towards the bureau and opened it. Her passport was the first object her eyes alighted on.

'My, what a delightful surprise!'

Lindy gripped the edge of the bureau, convinced that she was about to pass out with terror.

'I hope I'm right in thinking there could only be one reason for your presence in my room,' murmured Niko silkily, his tread as silent now, as he reached her violently trembling figure, as it had been when he had first entered the room. 'Why, Lindy, you seem cold!' he murmured, his arms enveloping her. 'Let me warm you— that's why you're here, isn't it?'

'Stop it!' she cried out, reaching out for her passport and pushing wildly against him.

The swiftness of the violence with which he spun her around, then slammed her against the wall, sent the breath exploding from her in a cry of terror.

'Well, well, what have we here?' he asked softly, trapping both her arms by the wrists and raising them high above her head, while his body moved towards her confining her completely. 'Trying to steal your passport? Now that's going to make me think you're not happy here with me,' he continued in that same relentlessly soft tone. 'Have I been neglecting you, Lindy? If so, I shall have to make amends, because we both know that in your heart of hearts you want to stay here with me— don't we, Lindy? You and I have so much unfinished business to attend to.'

'Yes, we have!' she croaked, her eyes tightly shut so that she wouldn't have to face the mockery in his in the face of her deliberate misinterpretation of his words. 'And soon I'll pay you back every penny of it!'

'Lindy, you misunderstand me,' he murmured. 'I've already told you the money is immaterial to me. But you know that anyway... just as you know exactly what the unfinished business between us is.'

She gave a choked squeal of protest as she felt the seductive warmth of his breath against her face, her body struggling wildly as his lips began nuzzling her cheek.

'Please, Niko, don't!'

'You have nothing to fear,' he whispered enticingly, drawing her trapped arms down to encircle his neck. 'I've told you I'd never force myself on you... and I never shall.'

'Niko, I... I lied to you!' she cried out disjointedly as the familiar melting softness began pervading her body. 'I love Tim! I didn't marry him on the rebound!'

The effect of those words was instant. He dragged her arms away from where he had placed them, his eyes black with fury in the sudden pallor of his face.

'Oh, yes?' he sneered. 'It's because you love him so much that you were beside yourself with worry when he ran off—is that what you're telling me?'

'No! I... I knew he'd gone... that he was all right,' she stammered. 'I... we'd quarrelled. And now he's forgiven me and he's sending the money to make up for what he did.'

'The usual way for making up for what he did is to spend time in prison,' retorted Niko coldly. 'And he can send as much money as he likes, but nothing will alter the fact that he lost you to me!'

'You're mad!' screamed Lindy, pushing against him with all her might and running for dear life as the suddenness of her move caught him momentarily off guard.

The fury with which he then reacted, grabbing hold of a handful of her dress and hauling her back towards him, sent her spinning off her feet as the material ripped beneath the tug of his hand.

She gave a scream of fear when she saw the edge of the chest of drawers looming towards her face and then a sharp cry of pain as the arm she had lifted in reflex protection took the full impact of her fall.

'Lindy—oh, God, I'm sorry!' he cried out, crouching down beside her and clasping her head in his hands. 'Something happens to me when I'm angry with you that makes me behave in a way I never have before! Your head could have been split open on that chest of drawers...when I grabbed you I'd no idea you'd fall as you did!'

Even as she opened her mouth to speak, Lindy was fighting against the words that would have come from her—words of forgiveness and understanding, rather than words of anger. But, as it was, any words she would have spoken caught soundlessly in her throat as her winded lungs greedily gasped in air.

'Lindy!' he groaned, then scooped her up in his arms and carried her over to the bed. 'What's wrong? Say something, for God's sake!' he exclaimed as he lay her gently down on the bed.

'I'm winded, for heaven's sake!' she managed to gasp.

The look of concern on his face faded to one of faint bemusement as he released her and sat down on the edge of the bed.

Lindy gazed up at him, feeling she was almost reading his mind. His concern had been genuine, but now he was regretting his spontaneous expression of it, she realised as his look of bemusement turned to one of resentment.

'In future, don't go nosing around where you've no right to be,' he stated icily, his expression now one of open hostility.

Her lungs now adequately filled, but her re-igniting fury rendering her speechless, Lindy began struggling upright, only to find herself prevented from doing so by his hands on her shoulders.

'Just who the hell do you think you are?' she shrieked. 'Let me up!'

'No,' he retorted, his eyes flickering dispassionately over her as he kept his hands firmly on her shoulders. 'I don't want you collapsing all over the place.'

'I'm perfectly all right and I want to get up!'

'Don't be silly,' he retorted blandly. 'You're as white as a sheet.' But a light had begun burning in his eyes that was nothing remotely resembling bland.

'And so would you be if some lumbering lout had tried to smash your head up against a chest of drawers!' she exploded, trying to counter the attack of his eyes with the lowest one she could come up with of her own, before the odd mixture of lethargy and excitement, now wending its disturbingly sensuous way throughout her, captured her completely.

'Lindy, I've told you that wasn't deliberate. And I apologise most profusely,' he said softly. 'But can't you understand how disconcerting, to say the least, it was

for me to find a woman in my bedroom, especially——?'

'Oh, yes?' she burst out before she could stop herself.
'And I'm sure you were disconcerted no end to find
Arista in here last night!' Even before his softly mocking
laughter had reached her ears she was berating herself
for not having bitten off her tongue rather than give vent
to that bitter outburst.

'It obviously upsets you—the idea of Arista being here
with me,' he taunted softly as he leaned over her, his
hands sliding down from her shoulders to her upper
arms.

'It doesn't upset me in the least!' lied Lindy ve-
hemently, her mind scrabbling for a means to salvage at
least the remnants of her pride. 'What infuriates me is
that ridiculous charade in which I was forced to partici-
pate——'

'Lindy, how many times do I have to tell you that I
never resort to force?' he sighed, his tone one of mockingly long-suffering patience.

'So you don't regard this as force?' she demanded.
'Or are you kidding yourself I'm here of my free will?'

'This is different—it's for your own good,' he murmured, his tone now parodying sweet reason. 'And as
for my kidding myself——'

'You mean if *you* decide it's for my own good *I* don't
have any say in the matter!' she retorted angrily. 'But
nothing can alter the fact that I'm not here by choice!'

'Aren't you, Lindy?' he asked, releasing her, his eyes
half hooded as they gleamed down into hers.

Fearful of the strange heat within her that had nothing
to do with anger, her gaze dropped from his to his mouth.
It was a strong, beautifully shaped mouth—one that
could be as seductive when it nuzzled teasingly as when

it bruised in passion. Her eyes darted back to his, filled with consternation at the very idea of such thoughts.

'I've released you, Lindy,' he breathed huskily.

'But you're still blocking my way,' she protested unevenly, the pounding of her heart making breathing almost an impossibility.

'I really was worried about you getting up too soon,' he told her softly, a somnolent darkness creeping into his eyes. 'Lindy, I can't explain why I lose my temper the way I do with you... Would you believe me if I told you that it frightens me almost as much as it must you?'

'Yes... but I shouldn't have been in here,' she whispered, barely conscious of what she was saying. 'I just had to have my passport.'

'So that you can return to the man you love!' he exclaimed, his expression hardening.

The 'no' was almost on her lips before she bit it back and closed her eyes to the ruthlessly probing gaze of the one and only man her perverse heart had chosen to love.

'Lindy, why does it seem to upset you—talking about the man you love?' he asked, his fingers reaching out to stroke against her cheek.

'Why are you doing this to me?' she cried out, her eyes flying open as she turned her face from the trespass of those fingers.

'Doing what to you, Lindy?' he enquired, suddenly rearranging his body till he lay outstretched beside her, his chin cupped in his hand as he gazed down at her from lazily enquiring eyes. 'I was merely——'

'You're merely playing!' she lashed out bitterly. 'Perhaps you enjoy slumming occasionally——'

'Slumming?' he echoed, aghast. 'You really do come out with some most baffling statements.'

He grabbed hold of her as she tried to roll to the other side of the bed.

'You know exactly what I mean!' she screamed at him, her fists pummelling furiously against him as he drew her back towards him. 'You're amusing yourself at my expense when you can obviously have your pick of women! There's Arista—who's obviously only too willing to——'

'I don't find any of this in the least amusing,' he informed her coolly, pinning her flailing arms to her sides. 'And I don't happen to want Arista, or any other——'

'That's certainly not the impression she, or any one else, would have formed last night! Let go of me!'

'Only when you stop having this ridiculous tantrum,' he informed her, laughing softly as he pulled her into his arms, 'and get it into that beautiful, though at times incredibly stupid head of yours that my problem is not Arista.' He gave a soft groan of exasperation, then buried his face against hers, his mouth hot and searching against her skin. 'My problem is you—wanting beyond all reason a woman whose eyes devour me, even as she's telling me she loves another man.'

She tried to fight as he drew her fully against him, then it became a fight against the fire leaping within her in answer to the urgent message of desire in the firm lean body ensnaring hers; and then it was a fight only to imprison him in her own arms and to answer the hot hunger of his mouth with the impassioned plea of her own.

As the heat grew to an unbearable pitch within her, there was no longer any relevance to her in the fact that hers was a love given with complete reluctance. Whatever its origins, it was now a love running wild, aching to express itself as it responded without restraint to the inciting caress of the hands now freeing her body of its clothing while they roved in impatient search.

'You're beautiful!' he cried out in hoarse exultation, his eyes devouring her nakedness as he impatiently stripped free of his own clothing.

Then his hands and his mouth were bombarding her body, awakening in it pleasures so acute that there was almost the sharpness of pain in them.

'Lindy, you're trembling,' he whispered, his lips brushing softly against hers while his hands swept the length of her body, rising to cup her breasts, where the tantalising play of his fingers against her aching flesh brought a soft, almost agonised cry bursting from her. 'Why are you trembling so?' he demanded huskily, raising his head from hers.

She shook her head, her mind blurred by the aching demands possessing her, her arms clinging tightly round his neck and drawing his head back to hers.

'Don't be so impatient,' he teased, laughter for a moment dancing in his eyes before they widened in surprise as she drew his head even further down and began pressing frantic little kisses against the faint scar gleaming on his forehead. 'Lindy, have you any idea how much I want you?' he groaned hoarsely, his mouth frantic against the straining tautness of her breasts as he buried his face against them.

She felt her hands tense against his back, her fingernails raking against its muscled smoothness as the slow play of his hands in intimate exploration against her body brought a softly panting cry to her lips.

He lifted his head again, this time his mouth returning to probe against hers.

'Don't be shy with me, Lindy,' he urged against her parted lips.

As though released by that impassioned plea, her hands slackened their fierce yet uncertain hold and began their own uninhibited exploration of the powerfully muscled body beneath them.

At first his response was a soft chuckle of delight, but it was as her eager hands grew bolder that she felt the same shivering tension that racked her own body send its shuddering ripples through his.

'It's all right, my darling,' he whispered as the need in her became too great and she simply clung to him, the salty sweetness of his skin on her lips as she cried out his name. 'It's all right,' he repeated, his mouth silencing her cries as his body stilled the wild undulations of hers.

She heard him call out her name in that bitter-sweet moment of pain and pleasure when his body invaded hers, a sound that deteriorated from exultation almost to anguish as a sharp cry of reflex protest burst from her. But no sooner had that initial cry escaped her than she was lost in the sweet madness of loving, her body abandoning itself with wanton fervour to the explosive force possessing it, responding with total lack of inhibition to each shock wave of pleasure bombarding it until she was crying out in incredulous protest. And her protests became wild sobs of love as pleasure soared to a mutual explosion of ecstasy between them and the hoarse cry of fulfilment torn from him, ultimately softened to huskily incoherent murmurings that whispered against her ear.

She was floating on a cloud from which nothing could ever dislodge her, she sang to herself, her mind still floating in that drugged realm of total fulfilment. Nothing mattered—nothing at all, save lying spent in the arms of the man she loved.

She folded her own arms more securely around him, her eyes misty with love as she gazed down at the dark, tousled head nestled against her breasts. And the love

within her was an exquisite ache, straining to be ac-
knowledged in words, just as it had in passionate action.
A passion such as she could never have come close to
imagining, she thought dreamily, a lazy smile creeping
to her lips as she wondered if he was actually going to
fall asleep without so much as a word of acknowledgement of the magic they had shared.

She sank her fingers into the vibrant silkiness of his
hair, starting as his head shook impatiently free from
her touch. Too lost in wonderment to be daunted, she
ran her fingers teasingly across the bronzed curve of his
shoulder, this time her eyes widening in shocked hurt as
he shrugged free of that touch too, his body suddenly
breaking all contact with hers as he flung himself away,
his head turned from her.

Lindy felt every functioning part of her body freeze
in shock, save for a tiny, almost pleading voice within
her denying that this could really be happening.

'I'm sorry,' he muttered, suddenly hauling himself up
on his elbows. 'I honestly had no idea you would be a
virgin.'

Lindy gazed down at the eyes that refused to meet
hers, her mind bombarding her with memories of what
they had just shared. As his eyes rose to hers it was their
stark coldness that made it impossible for her to equate
him with the frenzied lover of only moments before.

'How could you have known?' she asked hoarsely,
wondering where on earth she had found the words, let
alone the ability to utter them. 'You were under the impression I was a married woman.'

'Of course I wasn't,' he exclaimed harshly. 'I had my
suspicions right from the start...and then your passport
told me I was right.'

'I didn't think about that,' muttered Lindy numbly.

'There are a lot of things you didn't think about,' he exploded angrily. 'For God's sake, Lindy, I thought you'd been living with Russell!'

'Well, now you have your proof I wasn't!' she exploded back as something seemed to die in her.

'Do you think I'd behave as I did had I known?' he demanded, his voice hoarse with outrage.

'What difference can it possibly make whether you were the first or the fifty-first?' she retorted bitterly. 'You needn't have any fears about my father descending on you and demanding that you do the decent thing by his daughter, if that's what's bothering you!'

'The decent thing being to marry you—is that what you're saying?'

'No, of course it's not! All I meant——'

'You were the one to use the term "decent"!'

'It's an *expression* people use, for heaven's sake!' she groaned in disbelief. 'I honestly don't believe I'm hearing this!'

'What don't you believe you're hearing?' he demanded angrily. 'You can't seriously have expected me to make no comment! I'm not an irresponsible seducer who——'

'*I* also had some choice in what happened!' she flung at him in fury. 'The responsibility for what I do is mine, not yours!'

'Lindy, I was the first——'

'Only the first of many, if I have my way,' she cut in viciously, the savage hurt in her demanding retribution. 'So the fact that you were the first is no big deal, as far as I'm concerned. Some women are slow reaching sexual maturity—it was just your bad luck to be around when I reached mine!' Though not completely convinced that outburst had made much in the way of sense, she was almost boosted by it—until the unexpected sting of tears against her cheeks stripped her of even that and she turned away, wanting to curl up and wither away.

'You can say what you like, but——'

'Yes, I damned well can!' she choked. 'And what I'd like—what I intend doing—is to pay you what you're owed and get away from this place forever!'

'Lindy, you're crying!' he accused, rising and wrenching her round to face him.

'No, I'm not! But what I am doing is making a mental list of all the men I'll make love to now——'

'Lindy, stop it!' he ordered harshly, dragging her down beside him.

'Why should I?' she raged. 'You're not the only man in the world!'

'Damn you, Lindy! You...' He broke off with a soft groan of outrage as his body responded to the renewed proximity of hers with rampant enthusiasm.

'Damn you too, Niko,' choked Lindy in protest as her own body responded with an equally violent urgency.

'What was that you were saying about my not being the only man in the world?' he muttered barely coherently against her mouth as their bodies clung in an orgy of welcome.

'Did I say that?' she whispered distractedly, her lips nuzzling hungrily against his.

'Yes, but you didn't mean it,' he groaned, swift shudders of excitement surging through him as her body unequivocally told him that, for her, there could be no other man in the world but him.

CHAPTER NINE

'YOUR bedroom manners are appalling.'

Lindy emerged from beneath the covers, her cheeks flushed with sleep as she dragged herself up against the pillows and peered groggily at the man lounging, fully dressed, in the doorway of her bedroom.

'I beg your pardon?' she croaked, still not fully awake.

'I said—your bedroom manners are appalling,' repeated Niko, strolling towards the bed, his expression inscrutable as he gazed down at her.

As the veil of sleep drifted slowly from her mind, Lindy gave a soft groan, then rolled over and buried her head against the pillows. When her mind began to fill with memories of an overwhelmingly erotic nature she pulled the bedcovers up over her head.

'Lindy, what the hell are you doing?' demanded Niko, whipping back the covers.

'Go away and leave me alone!' Just the words with which she had always dreamed she would greet her lover on their first morning, she informed herself miserably, twitching her shoulder irritably as he gave it a sharp tap. 'Go away! Can't you see I'm dying of embarrassment?'

The bed sagged slightly as it took his weight.

'There's no need for you to start dying of embarrassment simply because I criticised your bedroom manners,' he chuckled.

Lindy turned and sat up.

'My God, I don't believe it! You're actually laughing!' she exclaimed sarcastically. 'I'm astounded that you're not still ranting on about...' She broke off, her cheeks scarlet as she realised what she had come so close to saying.

'About your lost virginity?' he prompted helpfully.

'And what do you mean—my bedroom manners are appalling?' she blurted out in her desperation to distract him.

'Lindy, it really is extremely bad form to sneak away—without so much as a word—as you did last night,' he chided.

'What was I supposed to do—leave a thank-you note?' she snapped, vowing to herself that this morning, of all mornings, there was no way she intended suffering a single word of sarcasm from him.

'That would have been a pleasant touch,' he murmured, both his expression and his words dead-pan. 'But what you really should have done was stay.'

'Oh, I do apologise,' she exclaimed with venomous sweetness. 'But then, I obviously don't have your vast experience in such matters!'

'Lindy, why did you leave me?' he demanded, his tone hardening with lack of amusement.

For the first time since he had entered the room Lindy looked into his face. She wished she hadn't, as her heart immediately attempted the impossible feat of turning wild somersaults while plummeting with despair. All she wanted was to be able to put her arms around him and pour out her love—instead she found herself glaring up into the uncompromising coldness of his eyes.

'Because, great though the sex was——' The forced flippancy of her words deteriorated into a sharp cry of fright as he jerked her head painfully back by the hair.

'Don't you dare try cheapening yourself with talk like that,' he rasped, his voice tight with fury.

'And I'd be the one cheapened, wouldn't I, Niko?' she flung back at him, a hollow chill aching its way through her. 'Because no one as perfect as you ever could be!'

'Lindy, stop this!'

'You're very good at telling others when to stop saying things,' she pointed out with bitter quietness. 'But not yourself. It didn't occur to you not to open your mouth and have your say last night.' As he released his painful grasp on her hair, she arched her knees and dropped her forehead against them. 'Why couldn't you have left well alone last night?' she intoned bitterly. 'Why hadn't you the grace to accept what had happened instead of spoiling it all by turning it into such a big production?'

A big production? she thought miserably. It had been the most momentous happening in her entire life...yet for him it would have been no more than another notch in a long series of conquests had it not been for this peculiar fixation of his regarding the loss of her virginity.

'Lindy, how can I not—as you put it—make a big production out of it?' he sighed, rubbing his hands wearily against his face. 'You have to understand that I regarded you as an experienced woman...one who would——'

'Oh, I understand all right!' she interrupted harshly, devastated by the implications behind his words. He was quite happy to have a brief fling with what he termed an experienced woman, but regarded her almost as a species apart and a potential danger! 'And you can rest assured that I'm not about to turn into a clinging vine and start making demands on you! Tim's money should arrive any day now—and when it does you'll be paid what you're owed and I shall be off!'

His only reaction was to sink his face fully into the hands he had been rubbing against it.

'And now, if you don't mind,' she stated brightly, even while her heart slowly shattered within her, 'I'd like to get up.'

'If you think I'm letting you go in a few days—you're mad!' he stated, straightening.

Though his words had been undeniably brusque, they sent hope staggering drunkenly through the aching chaos within her.

'My assumption that you were an experienced woman also carried with it the assumption that... Hell, Lindy, you could have become pregnant last night!' he groaned. 'And you can't avoid facing that fact by burying yourself under the bedclothes!' he exploded angrily as she made to do just that. 'Lindy, I accept that the fault was entirely mine—especially that second time,' he admitted hoarsely.

'Why didn't you take any precautions... that second time?' she asked dazedly, scarcely aware of what she was saying as her mind reeled in total confusion.

'Because... Lindy, do I really have to spell it out to you why?' he protested.

'Yes!' she insisted, something in his voice triggering off a driving need in her to know that his need for her had been every bit as destructively overwhelming as hers had been for him.

'Because you're the only woman I've ever known who has the power to make me lose my reason,' he stated abruptly, rising to his feet. 'Not that I regard that as any excuse at all!' He walked to the door. 'And perhaps now you'll understand why there's no way I can allow you to leave here until we both know for certain that you're not pregnant.'

'And what if I am?' she asked, the words bursting from her of their own volition.

'If you are then I'll have no choice but to do what you call the decent thing—I'll marry you.'

'Over my dead body!' shrieked Lindy, hurling a pillow at the door as it closed behind him.

She flung herself down against the remaining pillow, a violent paroxysm of sobbing racking her body. He wanted to keep her here—even to marry her under certain circumstances—but not because he loved her as she loved him! Oh, no—it was simply because he now saw her in the same sort of light that a farmer might regard a valuable brood mare!

It wasn't really stealing, Lindy told herself with little conviction. She patted the wad of notes bulging in one of the pockets of her jeans—notes she had taken from Niko's wallet.

Of course it wasn't stealing: her share of the money Tim had sent would more than cover it, she reasoned edgily. And if, as she had several times begged him to, Niko had arranged for the draft to be cashed she wouldn't have had to resort to this!

Several times resisting the strong temptation to glance back, she made her way to the small, secluded jetty. Today was to be the turning-point, she chivvied herself— today was the first day in a long while that luck had been consistently on her side. First there had been Niko's absence for the day and her finding his wallet on one of the chairs about an hour after his brusque announcement that he wouldn't be back until late.

Her shoulders hunched suddenly at the memory of the ghastly air of tension between them in the past few days, when any attempt at speech between them invariably ended in savagely bitter exchanges.

But that was all behind her now, she reminded herself as she turned down on to the path approaching the jetty.

Her second stroke of luck had been the arrival from the mainland of Vasilis's nephew. And she had handled that young man—the owner of a boat that could spell her freedom—rather well, she told herself in an effort to dispel those debilitating fears lurking so close to the surface of her mind. Unlike his uncle, Petros spoke some English and had met her casual enquiries as to what time he was leaving the island and whether he would object to a passenger with good-natured compliance. Her somewhat convoluted tale about contemplating some early Christmas shopping had over-taxed his limited English, but he had eventually appeared to have got the message that there was a possibility that she would join him, and he hadn't seemed to mind; nor, more to the point, had he shown any signs of suspicion.

She had killed the time until now in complete terror that Niko might arrive back earlier than he had indicated, she remembered with a shiver, then once again reminded herself that all that would be soon behind her as she stepped down on to the jetty.

Petros was nowhere in sight when she reached the small boat moored at the point of the jetty. She placed her holdall at her feet then glanced down at her watch, shivering slightly in the wind as she turned to glance back.

The sudden chilling of her bones to the marrow had nothing to do with the sharpness of the wind—it was the sight of the slight young man she awaited approaching along the path she had just taken, and that of the taller, more powerfully built Niko Leandros by his side.

For one crazy moment she actually contemplated leaping into the sea as a means of avoiding what she simply hadn't the will to face.

'I see you're taking a bag with you—to hold all your Christmas shopping, no doubt,' murmured Niko as the two men reached her, his eyes glittering fury as they alighted on the holdall by her feet.

Perhaps that was what she should have chucked into the sea, and then she could have claimed to be out for a walk, she thought gloomily—then told herself not to be so silly.

'Poor Vasilis was a bit anxious about your proposed trip to the mainland,' continued Niko icily. 'And I can't say I blame him—you're not dressed warmly enough, for a start.' He took hold of her by the arm, his fingers biting cruelly into her flesh. 'It's all right, Petros,' he said in slow, clear English. 'The young lady has decided to postpone her shopping until nearer Christmas.'

Petros nodded, murmured a reply in Greek, then flashed Lindy a slightly sheepish smile before leaping into his boat and roaring away. And well might he look sheepish, thought Lindy bitterly: she had made it as plain as she possibly could that her trip was to be a secret between the two of them—and he had told Vasilis, of all people!

'That wasn't a very clever move on your part,' Niko informed her angrily as he marched her back up to the hotel. 'You've no money, no passport—what the hell do you think you were playing at?'

'I was planning to go to the British Embassy in Athens for another passport,' she retorted, trying to prise his fingers from her arm without success. 'And as for money—I've plenty. I stole all there was in your wallet!'

'Obviously your time with Russell wasn't wasted,' he snapped, imperiously brushing her fingers aside as his grip on her arm, if anything, tightened. 'His penchant for thieving being one of the things you learnt from him.'

'I didn't really steal it,' she protested breathlessly, having almost to run to keep pace with his angry stride.

'I left you a note explaining . . . and another signing the entire bank draft over to you.'

'I can think of no word other than stealing for removing money that doesn't belong to you from another's wallet without his permission.' He marched her through the lobby and straight to the lift, his grip on her never once easing. 'As far as I'm concerned, the only place for people like you and Russell is behind bars!'

Fear flared like a flame in her, only to be quickly smothered by a surge of fury.

'Whatever Tim Russell has done has nothing to do with me!' she raged as he almost flung her through the door of the suite. 'And, if you hadn't refused to deal with that bank draft, I wouldn't have had to borrow any of your precious money!'

'The word is steal, Lindy!' he snarled, hurling her holdall across the room. 'And, as for your relationship with Russell, perhaps I should point out that, from a legal point of view, your not being his wife makes it far more likely that you'd be regarded as a willing accomplice rather than a coerced dependant.'

'Why do you suddenly feel the need to point that out to me?' she asked, her mouth suddenly uncomfortably dry.

'I'd have thought that was obvious,' he snapped. 'But I'll spell it out in case it isn't: if the only way I can guarantee your remaining here is to have you put behind bars—I shan't think twice about doing so. It's entirely up to you, Lindy.'

She didn't believe that he meant it, she told herself over and over, but doing so did nothing to lessen the panic clawing in the pit of her stomach.

'You wouldn't do that,' she croaked, her voice gaining confidence as she forced her mind to attempt func-

tioning logically. 'If you did and it turns out I am
pregnant your child would be born in prison.'

'Are you prepared to risk testing me on whether I'd
let that happen?' he asked, his words sounding so suddenly vague that she glanced up at him in puzzlement.

He turned away from her, his face contorting slightly
as he screwed his eyes tightly shut.

'Niko?' she queried uncertainly. 'Niko, what's wrong?'
she gasped, reaching out to him as he gave an angry
shake of his head and immediately began swaying on his
feet.

He shrugged free of her, his gait almost reeling as he
made his way to the sofa and flung himself down on it.

'Damn, damn, damn!' he groaned softly, pressing his
hands to his temples.

'Right—I'm getting a doctor!' exclaimed Lindy, sick
with fright as she raced over to the telephone.

'I don't need a doctor!' he exclaimed irritably.

'Of course you do!' she protested, her voice high-
pitched with fear as she lifted the receiver.

'Lindy, put that bloody thing down!' he roared. 'I'm
not a fool—if I needed a doctor I wouldn't hesitate to
summon one.' Startled by the aggression in his tone, she
dropped the receiver and flew to his side.

'Niko, what's wrong with you?' she asked, her tone
pleading.

'Nothing's the matter with me,' he retorted irritably.

'If you won't tell me I'll have no option but to ring
down to Maria and ask her to call a doctor.'

'Stop droning on about doctors,' he snapped, his eyes
once again clamping tightly shut. 'I know what's happening and it's my own fault. Mind you,' he added with
morose accusation, 'that little performance of yours can't
have helped.'

Lindy glanced down at him in appalled uncertainty. He didn't seem to be making any sense...perhaps he was having some sort of a seizure!

'Niko, are you epileptic?'

He shook his head, a lop-sided, faintly surprised smile sneaking to his lips.

She sat down, wedging herself beside him.

'Niko, you're frightening me...please tell me what's happening,' she pleaded.

'It's no big deal,' he muttered wearily. 'I've been having bouts of double vision on and off since the accident—that's why I've been subjected to this prolonged convalescence.'

'How often does it happen?'

'That's the infuriating thing about it—I hadn't had it for a couple of weeks and thought I was over it. The doctors said it would gradually disappear, but until it did so I was to vegetate.'

'I'm sure they didn't put it quite like that,' murmured Lindy, the sickening tension that had gripped her slackening with relief.

'Not being able to work—or read, even—is the same as vegetating, as far as I'm concerned,' he informed her morosely. 'Not only do I read a lot for pleasure, but running a multi-faceted business such as mine entails a mountain of technical reading.' He took a couple of cushions and wedged them under his head. 'This morning I decided I'd had enough of being a damned invalid and took myself off to my Athens office.'

'You went back to work today—in Athens?' gasped Lindy.

'That's what I've just said, isn't it?' he exclaimed irritably.

'What did your doctors say when you had your medical the other day?' she asked—a question she hadn't even been able to put to him, given the hostile nature of their recent exchanges.

'They said I had to accept that I need more time before I think of starting work again,' he snapped. 'And if you have any comments to make on that score I'd rather you kept them to yourself!'

'But you'd already been doing paperwork here,' she snapped, determined to have her say, 'winding up the hotel.' Then, softening, she added wryly, 'Anyway, Niko, a couple of months' rest is hardly too much to ask for the sake of your health.'

'I suggest you try it some time,' he retorted belligerently, 'then, perhaps, you'd be more qualified to judge!'

'For heaven's sake, listen to you!' she snapped. 'You don't seem to realise how fortunate you are! Just because——' She clamped her lips tightly shut, unable to believe she had just been about to mention Arista's abandonment of him right after his accident.

He tried to struggle upright, then flopped back wearily, crooking his arm across his eyes.

'What are you trying to tell me, Lindy?'

'Nothing—it's just that you don't seem to appreciate what you have,' she replied wearily. 'Your looks——'

'What have looks to do with it?' he cut in scathingly. 'Tell me, Lindy, as an exceptionally beautiful woman, exactly what do looks have to do with anything?'

'Nothing!' she retorted hotly. 'But you've always been good-looking and it would have been hard for you to have lost your looks. And, if they mean so little to you, why do you refer to mine with such exaggeration—or were you simply being sarcastic?'

He lowered his arm, his eyes hooded, almost closed, as he looked at her. 'Sarcastic? Damn it, you *are* beautiful!'

'I was a fat and ugly teenager!' she rounded on him accusingly. 'I am now an averagely good-looking adult, and for that I'm more than grateful. And what I don't need is well-meaning and exceptionally good-looking people, such as my parents and my sister—and men like you—feeling duty-bound to make exaggerated claims about my looks in order to boost my self-confidence!'

His expression was now one of complete horror.

'My God, I can hardly believe this—you sound almost unbalanced! Have you reacted like this on other occasions when men have told you you're beautiful?'

'Don't men usually tell women they're beautiful when they try to lure them into their beds?' she asked bitterly.

'Only the fools,' he replied quietly. 'Lindy, I know looks mean far more to most people than they should do and it's a fact that I often find sickening. But I can assure you that, no matter how fat a little girl you were, you were beautiful then, just as you're a very beautiful woman now.' He grasped her by the arms. 'And I have no doubt that several men have tried to lure you into their beds with lies . . . but I can assure you that not one single one of them was lying when he told you that you're beautiful. And if you can't accept that you have a problem,' he finished as he gently released her.

'A problem?' she echoed, knowing that the most beautiful woman in the world could never have felt this good.

'A mighty big problem. The two women I see before me are as beautiful as any I'm ever likely to see, and all I can say is God knows what sort of ravishing creatures their parents and sister are if they rate themselves average by their standards!'

When he began speaking Lindy was regarding him with frowning alarm—by the time he had finished she was laughing weakly.

'Niko, I'm sorry—it's not in the least funny,' she apologised as he flopped back down against the cushions, 'but can you really see two of me?'

'They're overlapping a bit,' he replied, 'but yes—I can.'

'But the doctors *are* sure it's definitely nothing serious?' she exclaimed, her eyes dropping in sudden consternation as he raised mockingly enquiring eyebrows in response to the undisguised anxiety unconsciously entering her words.

'I've had brain scans and every other test there is— and no, grossly irritating though this is, serious it isn't,' he told her, his tone soft with amusement. 'But tell me,' he continued, bringing a swift rush of colour to her cheeks by placing a hand over one of hers, 'how exactly do you feel about the possibility of carrying a child of mine?'

Lindy snatched away her hand, thrown not as much by the complete unexpectedness of the question as by the almost casual indifference with which it had been put.

'Such enthusiasm,' he mocked, then gave a soft laugh that chilled her blood. 'And so ironic—when I think of the women I know who would be only too happy to be in your shoes right now.'

'You're despicable!' she whispered hoarsely, her agitated attempts to return to her feet halted by his hands descending heavily to her hips.

'What's so despicable about stating the truth?' he asked. 'I'm thirty and single, the sole heir to the empire whose name I bear, and a fairly wealthy man by most standards. I can't think of many who wouldn't agree I was a pretty good catch...though, of course, there could be the odd nasty-minded person around who might entertain the thought that you had angled for me and landed me with superb skill.'

Lindy could almost feel the colour draining from her face as she gazed at him beseechingly.

'Niko, you can't possibly believe that!' she pleaded.

'Oh, but I could—possibly,' he mocked with a shrug of indifference.

'Well, you're mad!' she exclaimed, her temper flaring hotly. 'Because, even if I were carrying triplets of yours, you'd still be the last person on this earth I'd ever even contemplate marrying!'

'The number is immaterial, and you wouldn't have any option!'

'That's where you're so very wrong,' she hurled at him, twisting furiously in an attempt to break free. '*If* I have the misfortune of being pregnant—which is a very big "if"—one option I do have is not to continue being so!'

There had been something recoiling in her so violently from what she was saying that she couldn't bring herself to use specific words—but the howl of outrage emitting from Niko as he sat up and dragged her face to face with him told her that he had no doubts whatever as to what she had implied.

'They say that power corrupts,' he told her in softly venomous tones, his face scant inches from hers, 'a saying that's never been true concerning a Leandros. Be warned, though, that this is one Leandros who would use his power to pull every string he had to, and more, to get his own way. I'll keep you in chains, if necessary, and once you've had that child I'll make certain that you leave this country and never return to it again...and I guarantee you would never see the child at all!'

'Niko, please...this is ludicrous!' she protested, appalled by the severity of his reaction. 'We don't even know that I *am* pregnant, for heaven's sake! In fact, I feel certain I'm not.'

'Now who's being ludicrous? How can you possibly feel certain?' he demanded savagely. 'But, for your sake, I hope to God that you're not pregnant!'

He flung her aside so violently that she almost fell from the sofa, then leapt to his feet, charging unsteadily away from her.

Her heart in her mouth as she watched him, she tried to steel herself against the rush of protective love flooding her and demanding that she go to his aid by telling herself that it was only temper making him charge around like that and exacerbating his problems.

She winced as he stumbled into the side of a small table and kicked it angrily from his path, and she winced yet again when the door of his room slammed vibratingly shut.

She lay back against the sofa and closed her eyes, wondering how many times it had been in the past weeks that she had told herself she had had enough and could take no more. This time she had truly reached rock-bottom . . . there was no further down she could go.

She hadn't known it, of course, but until she had fallen in love she hadn't had a care in the world, she thought bitterly. And love had turned her into a pathetic cry-baby, she thought furiously as her eyes filled and overflowed. Niko had told her she was beautiful and for the first time in her life she had felt she was . . . but if she had the choice between love and feeling fat and ugly she certainly wouldn't choose love!

As a choked sob escaped her she tried to shake off the desolation gripping her by reminding herself that in about ten days' time she would at least know whether or not she was pregnant—only to hear Niko's last words echo savagely in her head.

'...for your sake, I hope to God that you're not pregnant!'

The heavy sound of something smashing brought her leaping to her feet and racing into Niko's room.

'Niko, what on earth...?' Her words petered to a shocked halt. He was standing by the bed, the coldness of hatred dulling his eyes as they flickered towards her and one of the beautiful, heavy marble lamps that stood on either side of it lying strewn in pieces across the floor.

'I knocked into the lamp,' he informed her in a curiously flat tone.

Her mind recoiling sickeningly from that expression she had glimpsed in his eyes, she glanced down at the pieces littering the floor—of a lamp obviously hurled with violent intent—and then to the man by the bed, his eyes now dazed and blank.

Lindy shook her head in utter bemusement as love suddenly hit her with the impact of a vicious blow, negating all within her save love itself.

'Niko, I'm sorry,' she blurted out, knowing that had she been able to she would have been unwilling to hold back the words anyway. 'I didn't mean what I said...I'd no right to upset you when you were feeling so ghastly.'

He sat down on the edge of the bed as she went to his side, his face drawn and exhausted.

'What would you have done—saved it until I was feeling better?' he asked bitterly, confusing her utterly by leaning forward and resting his face against her. 'And you can rest assured that I meant every word I said.'

Of their own volition her hands rose to his head, gently caressing his hair, love and anguish tearing her apart as she tried to blot from her mind that terrible look of hatred that had been in his eyes.

'I especially meant what I said about your being beautiful,' he added, linking his arms lightly around her and raising his face to hers. 'And most especially what I said the other day—about your being the one woman capable of making me lose my reason.'

'Niko?' she exclaimed anxiously as he suddenly blinked hard.

'All of a sudden I'm getting short measure—I'm only seeing one of you now,' he muttered with the ghost of a relieved smile.

'Perhaps my stroking your head helps,' she said in a breathy, distorted voice.

'I can't say I'm finding it in the least soothing—but do continue,' he added swiftly when she removed her hands. 'That's better,' he murmured contentedly as she immediately returned them. 'But you do realise, I hope, that I'm finding your ministrations exceedingly stimulating.'

She gave a gasp of surprise as he suddenly pulled her against him, locking his legs around hers, a gasp that deepened to a soft moan of helplessness as his hands began sliding slowly up her body.

'But then, stimulating is what I've found you from the start,' he whispered huskily, drawing her head down to his. 'What we've always found one another right from the start, even though I was eminently more skilled at disguising what was happening to me than you ever were.'

The impassioned plea of his lips on hers was disrupting her ability to give his words the attention something deep within her felt they somehow warranted. She tried to draw back from the fierce onslaught of his mouth, his name exploding from her in a confused cry of welcome and uncertainty.

'Niko...why——?'

'No...please, Lindy,' he protested hoarsely, lifting her against him and rolling their entwined bodies over on to the bed, 'no whys...just love me!'

And there was an edge of desperation in the intensity with which she answered his plea, acknowledging that the love she so unstintingly gave was a love far removed from the one-dimensional emotion his desire had driven him to demand of her.

CHAPTER TEN

'I'M PLEASED to be able to say your bedroom manners have improved.'

Lindy's eyes flickered open from sleep and straight up into the golden-flecked darkness of Niko's, gazing down into hers.

He was standing by the bed, a navy tracksuit emphasising the lean athleticism of his body as he towelled dry his hair.

She dragged herself up on an elbow, the languorous excitement churning heavily within her suddenly dissipated by anxiety at the sight of his unnatural pallor and the almost bruised darkness around his eyes.

'Niko—are you feeling all right?' she whispered, suddenly wishing desperately that she were one of those people who woke to instant alertness instead of taking the ages she did to come round fully from sleep.

'I'm feeling fine,' he replied, sounding slightly taken aback. 'In fact, I've been for a swim,' he added, dropping the towel from his head to around his shoulders.

'I'd have loved to have joined you,' she protested with the unguarded candour of one still not fully awake. 'Why didn't you wake me?'

'You looked so peaceful,' he muttered, his expression suddenly hardening. 'And besides—I wanted to be on my own.'

Lindy was as fully awake now as though she had just leapt into the pool. Perhaps one of these days she would learn not to leave herself open to such crushing put-downs, she told herself bitterly, anger and hurt churning sickeningly inside her as he turned and walked to the door.

'But I'm glad you didn't take off and leave me in the night,' he muttered as he opened the door. 'I'll have breakfast sent up.'

For several seconds Lindy's eyes remained on the door that had just closed behind him as though mesmerised by it. Then she flung back the bedclothes, marched to the bathroom and turned on the shower.

Never in a million years would she understand how his mind worked, she told herself frustratedly... never! If he was so glad that she had stayed all night, why had he rejected the idea of her company in the pool? If she had made such an almighty impact on him from the first time they had met, how was it that he had always treated her with such cold condescension?

He had initially regarded her as married, she pointed out to herself as she stepped out of the shower—then shook her head in total confusion... at some time he had learned she wasn't and had then, if anything, treated her even worse!

She went to her own room and got dressed, telling herself that what it all boiled down to was that they were poles apart—that she would never understand him. And trust her, she added to herself in savage accusation, to fall in love with a man with whom she was totally incompatible! Suddenly she was meeting her own eyes reflected in the mirror and seeing the torrid heat flooding her cheeks. There was one area in which they were totally and magically compatible, her senses reminded her, and the knowledge filled her with a confusing mixture of elation and despair.

She turned disconsolately and left the room, the only clear thought in her head being that if she didn't get away from here soon she would end up an emotional and mental wreck.

Niko was on the telephone when she entered the room and, even though his words were unintelligible to her, she sensed their edgy abruptness as he terminated the conversation.

'Is anything wrong?' she asked, and was immediately annoyed with herself for voicing her reflex concern.

'I hope this isn't a symptom of pregnancy,' he snapped, rising to his feet and glowering at her, 'this sudden concern of yours that everyone and everything be all right.' He marched to the door. 'I shan't be joining you for breakfast when it arrives—I have visitors.'

The murderous rage which filled her as the door slammed shut behind him so frightened her that she had raced to her room and changed into her swimming things without any true consciousness of what she was doing.

But that was what she needed, she told herself grimly as she stepped into the lift, to swim herself into a state of utter exhaustion—because if she didn't the odds were that Niko Leandros would end up a corpse before the day was through!

The sight that met her eyes, as the lift doors swung open, was that of Niko walking towards the office—deep in conversation with a uniformed police officer. The breath solidified in her lungs as she caught sight of a second uniformed figure standing by the reception desk.

Her hands shaking uncontrollably, she slammed them against the button for the top floor, almost collapsing against the wall as she was carried upwards.

He had wanted to be alone this morning, she reasoned frantically—alone to plot exactly how she was to be dealt with! Almost staggering back to her room, she found herself remembering his edginess as he had terminated his telephone call the moment she had appeared—an action she now saw as a spontaneous gesture of guilt because there was no way she could have understood a word of what he had been saying.

She leaned her head against the smooth wood of the door, willing the feverish fear within her to subside enough for her to attempt rational thought. But, instead of subsiding, the fear took on a more solid form, centring on the angry exchanges of the night before and on the threats made with equal savagery on both sides.

Shaking her head from side to side as though trying to deny it, she remembered the threat she had made— one so abhorrent to her that she had hedged in her expressing of it ... but one Niko would make her pay for a thousand times over for having even hinted at.

And the fear within her swelled to a full-blown terror, driving her as she changed into jeans and a heavy sweater, screaming at her that there was no time to be wasted as she stuffed toiletries and a change of underwear into a large wash-bag, and interfering with the mobility of her legs as she tore down the back stairs and furtively made her way from the building.

He had asked her to love him and she had done literally that ... in return he planned to have her incarcerated.

She tried to drag her mind free from its entanglement of fear and recrimination and to concentrate on her first few weeks here, when she had explored the island extensively. She had automatically started heading north, but now doubled back, giving the hotel and its grounds a wide berth. There was far more territory northwards, she reasoned, and that was where anyone looking for her would search—but she had discovered two derelict cottages, and it was to the furthest of those that she drove her dementedly racing feet.

The sound of her own breath rasping in her lungs forced her to drop her wild dash to a less punishing jog. As her rhythm steadied she pushed her mind to examine this irrational fear within her—one ruthlessly suppressed since Tim's taunt of gaol had first germinated it—that, now unleashed, drove her like one possessed. And it was a totally irrational fear, she strained to convince herself. Had it not been for it she would have done the only sensible thing and called Niko's bluff. The whole idea of what he was doing was outrageous—absolutely outrageous! She could ring the British Embassy . . . she could ring her father, for heaven's sake! She was out of her mind, running like this!

Her jogging steps slowed to a walk . . . but running away as she was doing was tantamount to an admission of guilt, she reasoned numbly, panic rearing up in her to drive her on harder until, by the time she reached only the first of the cottages, she was staggering from exhaustion.

She sank to her knees on the dusty stone-flagged floor, promising herself that she would continue to the second cottage once she had had a rest; then she curled up and fell into an exhausted sleep.

She dreamt she was on Petros's small boat, the faint sound of the engines in her ears and the sea breeze on her face as she sped away to freedom. Later the sound of the engines was no longer with her and there was only the soft promise of freedom blowing gently against her face.

It was later still that she awoke, fear stirring druggedly in her as she realised that the sea breeze was in fact a draught coming in through the now partially opened door.

Her every muscle screaming in protest as she tried to sit up, she froze to immobility when she found herself suddenly gazing straight into the eyes of the man sitting beside her on the dusty floor, his chin resting on the arms hugging his arched knees.

'You frightened me,' Niko said, the only expression emanating from his still body contained in the controlled tightness of his words. 'I thought at first that you'd taken one of the boats.'

Lindy sensed the fear in her biding its time till it would explode into an orgy of pure terror. But the explosion that came, as those opening words of his reverberated in her head, was one of devastating anger.

'*I* frightened *you*!' she whispered hoarsely, the need in her to lash out and wound as she had been wounded superceding all fear. 'Oh, no, it's what you believe might possibly be growing within me that's frightened you... and rightly so! But it's too late, Niko, because, if it exists, it will never survive what lies in store for me!'

'What have you done?' he groaned, leaping up and dragging her to her feet after him.

'It's not what I've done—it's what you've done! Why do you think I stayed here? Do you honestly think that I'm so stupid, so weak-willed that I wouldn't have risked calling your bluff, no matter what the consequences?'

'So tell me, Lindy,' he asked tonelessly, turning away from her, 'what did keep you here?'

'Fear... no, not fear.' She shook her head, angry with her own indecisiveness. 'Now that I'm having to face it, I can only describe it as a blind, irrational terror.'

He swung round to face her once more, horror and uncertainty mingled on his features. 'A terror of what, for God's sake?'

'You're the one who's threatened me with it so often and so effectively—I'm surprised you ask,' she replied with a bitter laugh, stumbling past him and out into the brightness of the sunlight. 'So let's get it over and done with, Niko; I'm sure the police don't like to be kept waiting.'

'Lindy, I didn't bring the police here...' He broke off, putting out a hand to her as she slumped suddenly against the wall of the cottage, laughing weakly. 'For God's sake, Lindy!' he pleaded, his face racked with anxiety as he helplessly dropped his hand.

'I heard it in my dream,' she giggled, gazing at the Range Rover parked at a careless angle beside the crumbling stone wall in front of the cottage. 'I thought it was the engine of Petros's boat!'

He took her gently by the shoulders and turned her towards him.

'Lindy, is it the thought of going to prison that fills you with such fear?' he asked hoarsely.

'You know it is.' Though her body had turned, her head was still twisted towards the Range Rover, as though mesmerised by the sight of it.

'Lindy, I didn't summon the police here this morning—they were searching all the islands for someone who escaped from their custody on the mainland.'

'He probably didn't like the idea of being incarcerated either,' she sighed, then added with bitterness, 'But at least they won't be leaving here empty-handed.'

'They've already left—they had a radio message to say he'd been found.'

At those words she turned and faced him, her expression guarded and uncertain, but she said nothing.

'Lindy, I simply don't understand...it's not as though you have any problem with lifts or other confined spaces!' he exclaimed.

'Of course I don't!' she said, her face screwing up with puzzlement.

'So you're not claustrophobic.'

'I didn't say I was!'

'But...' He let out a confused exclamation, shaking his head in bewilderment as his hands dropped from her shoulders. 'But this terror you say you have of prison...' His words petered to a halt.

'I don't *say* I have it,' she whispered, closing her eyes to examine the monster lurking within her, its savage immediacy suppressed, but the threat of its full potential still growling in abeyance. 'It's a part of me... yet I was never even aware of its existence.'

'Lindy, mine was an empty threat... I would never, under any circumstances, ever have even considered having you sent to prison. And it was a threat I can only hope you will believe I would never have made had I had the slightest inkling of how it would have affected you. Lindy,' he pleaded raggedly, 'all I ask is that you tell me you believe that... Can you?'

Her eyes still closed, she nodded, unwilling to trust herself to speak and unable to comprehend how a fear so ungovernable could be erased with such totality, simply by the utterance of a few words...words in which she had implicit faith. 'Yes, I can,' she said, suddenly finding words, even as her head reeled in disbelief that such a swift and total removal of that mind-sapping, destructive terror could have left her with no more than this strange, inexplicable feeling of emptiness. 'Niko, I——'

'No,' he interrupted instantly. 'No more talking until you've had time to unwind from this unspeakable ordeal I've put you through.' The touch of his hand on her shoulder was no more than a brief guiding tap, steering her in the direction of the Range Rover. 'We'll go back to the hotel and tomorrow I'll arrange for you to be taken to the mainland and your flight back to London to be booked.'

The hotel appeared deserted when they reached it.

'You'll want some time on your own,' he said, leaving her as she entered the lift. 'Are you hungry?'

Lindy shook her head.

'Perhaps you'll feel like something later—after you've had a bath... You look cold.'

She nodded, wanting to say something, but finding no words. And then the lift doors glided closed.

She felt an empty, waiting stillness in her that was like the deathly calm preceding the most destructive of storms. Then the realisation came to her that this deathly calm was all she had... there would be no more storms.

She took a long bath and found that it had neither relaxed nor warmed one iota of the bone-deep chill in her.

She was standing gazing out through the closed balcony doors across the grey, foam-flecked sea when she heard the door open and knew instinctively that it was Niko.

'I didn't mean to disturb you,' he apologised. 'I... Lindy, why didn't you explain the phobia you have about prison to me? Did you honestly think I could be such a sadist?' he added, an empty starkness in his words.

'No,' she whispered, dropping her forehead against the coldness of the glass: she could never have thought that of him because it was the essential decency and compassion she had recognised in him that had led her to love him. 'Niko, how could I possibly explain it to you when I still don't even understand it myself? I wasn't even conscious that there was anything like that in me until Tim mentioned that I could end up in gaol... and then it was only a vague shadow at the back of my mind . . . it was something I was almost able to suppress until I was forced to face it . . . then it just seemed to overwhelm me.'

'Russell?' he exclaimed, his harsh utterance of that name coming from beside her. 'How could he possibly threaten you with imprisonment?'

'He said you could have me thrown in gaol if I confessed that he and I weren't married and had come here under false——'

'You can't possibly believe Greek law would be that harsh,' he interrupted, aghast.

'I know nothing about such laws . . . but that's precisely what you threatened to do, isn't it?' she replied, a terrible desolation now seeping into the void within her.

'Yes . . . it was,' he conceded hoarsely. 'But you're not afraid any more—are you, Lindy?'

She shook her head, unable to trust herself to speak as she suddenly saw clearly that, had she only trusted in the love her heart had chosen, no terror could ever have touched her.

'And you do trust me when I tell you that you'll be taken to the mainland tomorrow and your flight back to London will be arranged?'

'Yes,' she whispered barely audibly as the terrible emptiness seemed to settle into permanence within her.

'I wanted to clarify that between us because I want you to know with absolute certainty that those arrangements are not dependent on your answer to the question I'm about to ask you.'

For the first time since he had entered the room Lindy turned to where he stood beside her and looked at him, knowing with no shadow of a doubt what that question would be.

'Niko, if I am pregnant I shall have the child—there isn't and never was any question in my mind about that, no matter what I might have tried to imply.'

He leaned forward, resting his forehead against the glass just as she had hers moments before.

'I suppose I really hadn't any right to ask,' he stated hoarsely.

'You have every right to ask,' she replied firmly, love aching within her at sight of his almost gaunt pallor. Whatever the terrors he had resurrected in her, she now knew that there were those of an equal ferocity that she had created in him.

'Would you marry me if I asked you to?' he asked harshly.

'No!' she exclaimed, her voice as harsh as his as she had a sudden and vivid picture of the heartache with which her life would be filled as the wife of a man such as he—trapped in a marriage he would never have voluntarily chosen.

'Would you let me see the child?'

'How could I possibly deny either of you that?' she asked, the desolation so stark in her voice that he turned, frowning, to face her.

'Naturally I shall finance both you and the child.'

'Niko—we don't even know if I'm pregnant!' she protested.

'But if you are? You say you wouldn't deny me my child—but what if you married? I don't want you marrying for security!'

'If I wanted to marry for financial security I'd have said I'd marry you if it came to it!' she exclaimed exasperatedly.

'I'll set up a trust for both of you——'

'Niko, I don't want your money, for heaven's sake!'

'I'm not having any child of mine brought up as a pauper!' he retorted hotly.

'All right—have it your own way!' she cried, clamping her hands to her ears. 'Why does it always have to be a shouting match whenever we try to discuss anything?'

'You're right!' he exclaimed, the total unexpectedness of his capitulation throwing her completely. 'Perhaps it has something to do with the fact that we simply don't know one another!' he exploded exasperatedly. 'You don't know me! There are times when I don't even know myself any more!' He grabbed her suddenly by the hand and led her to the sofa. In a complete daze, Lindy followed, obediently sitting down beside him when he motioned her to do so. 'Can you understand that there have been times when it's almost as though I've stepped out of myself... and watched in horror the abusive, violent stranger I've just vacated?' he continued distractedly.

'Niko, I've always known that wasn't you,' she protested.

'How could you?' he demanded harshly. 'It's the version of me with which you're most familiar!'

'I just knew,' she repeated doggedly: she knew because she loved him.

For an instant the conviction in her words threw him, and for one terrible moment she found herself wondering if she hadn't spoken her silent rider aloud.

'Well, I, unfortunately, haven't your insight,' he informed her harshly. 'I have no idea of who the real Lindy is... hell, I don't even know what brought you here, let alone why you came posing as Russell's wife!'

There was something so oddly close to desperation in his words that she instantly responded by answering him. At first her words were strained and disjointed, then gradually she managed to relax marginally.

'With me in hospital after my uncle's death, the Leandros Corporation mandarins, not knowing what plans, if any, I had in mind for this place, thought the best thing to do was go ahead with my uncle's management recruitment,' he responded when she had finished. 'Unfortunately the only application they turned up was Russell's—the old boy had odd filing methods. They took it Russell had been his choice, so merely conducted token interviews and hired him. Other papers came to light some time later, making it plain that Russell's was the one application he had rejected out of hand.'

'I did often wonder about his qualifications,' murmured Lindy, 'though, to my completely amateur eyes, he seemed to have coped all right.'

'So it appeared—though I've a feeling the staff were perfectly capable of running the place without a manager overseeing them,' replied Niko. 'I didn't learn of the mistake that had been made until after I'd arrived here, so I had him thoroughly checked out. There was nothing on any record against him. And neither, to my relief, was there any record of his having married ... though it wasn't until I saw your passport that I felt able to accept that fact totally.'

Lindy glanced up at him, then quickly away as she felt the colour flood her cheeks.

'Why do you blush?' he drawled. 'I've already admitted the effect you had on me—it came as very much of a relief to discover I wasn't lusting after a married woman after all.'

'Yet the fact that you weren't absolutely certain I wasn't married didn't stop you arranging to win me in a poker game,' she retorted bitterly, any feelings of relaxation she might have had deserting her completely.

'Because I didn't feel easy about Russell I made sure I knew everything he was up to. And the unpleasant fact is that it was only a matter of time before word got through to his gambling companions of the beauty of his wife and they talked him into staking you. He didn't exactly show reluctance when I suggested it.'

'So now you're claiming you did it to protect me?' she asked, prompted by the bitterness engulfing her.

'Would it make you feel better if I said yes?' he enquired, his words accompanied by a cynical laugh.

'Not particularly,' she retorted, cut to the quick and hating herself for feeling so. 'It's just that I wondered if you made a habit of chivalrous acts—or wasn't it a question of chivalry, your forgiving Arista for having deserted you when she thought you were likely to lose your leg?' she added maliciously.

'You wouldn't have deserted me, would you, Lindy?' he murmured, then gave a chuckle that took her completely by surprise. 'To be honest, there was never any question of my losing a leg,' he said. 'The surgeon's observation that I was damned lucky not to have done so somehow got its way back to the compassionate Arista in a somewhat garbled version... I simply elicited the help of a few of the doctors in ensuring she didn't hear the correct version.'

'That was cruel!' gasped Lindy.

'Why cruel?' he demanded. 'What Arista fancied was wealth and position on the arm of a man her friends would envy her—predictably she didn't envisage them envying her a man she would consider decoratively useless, and therefore she couldn't get away from me fast enough.'

'No one could be that shallow,' protested Lindy, though, from her limited knowledge of Arista, she wasn't entirely sure.

'I've known Arista since we were children, and I can assure you she could be and is. Her family went down in the world when her father lost his money, and her one aim in life is to find herself a husband who can restore her to what she considers her rightful position.'

'So why on earth did you let her come back here?' asked Lindy.

'Quite simply because, in her own inimitable way, Arista managed to put it to me that if I didn't agree to her coming here she would make sure my parents got to hear of the accident. And, before you ask, no—it wasn't Arista that they eventually heard from.'

A picture of Arista in his arms swam before her eyes. His words about her might be disparaging, she thought bitterly, but his actions told a different tale.

'I still don't see why you needed me to pose as the woman in your life,' she muttered, her gaze, as it had been for several minutes now, trained on her lap.

'As I said, I've known Arista since we were children. I honestly felt she would have known better than to switch her predatory attentions to me—but, as there was no particular woman in my life at the time, I suppose she thought she might as well have a try. As for your role, one thing I do know about her is that her pride would come to my rescue—Arista would never risk losing face in front of a rival.'

'You talk about pride and losing face,' said Lindy woodenly. 'Don't you and your friends ever think in terms of love?'

'Surely it's a form of love that makes me protect Arista from herself,' he stated quietly.

'Well, if that's the case, why don't you do both of you a favour and marry the woman?' exploded Lindy unthinkingly, leaping from the sofa, her mind now swamped by those memories of another time—when he had held Arista in his arms scant feet away from where she now stood.

'Now who's turning it into a shouting match?' he asked, his eyes oddly expressionless as they rose to hers.

'At least I'm reacting honestly,' she flung back at him bitterly. 'Can't you understand that you don't have to smarm round me, pretending you're at last being honest? I've already told you that, if I *am* having your child, you can have as much access to it as you wish. So stop this ridiculous charade—it simply isn't necessary!'

'I wouldn't know how to smarm, even if I wanted to,' he retorted harshly, getting to his feet—at which point Lindy turned and fled.

She raced to her room and flung herself down on her bed, pummelling her fists against the pillows in an orgy of mindless despair.

'Get out of here!' she choked hysterically as she heard the door open, then buried her face in the pillows when she felt the bed take his weight.

'Lindy, you don't seem to understand that I can't afford the luxury of honesty,' he told her quietly. 'Because whatever I say you'll misinterpret my motives. And besides,' he added, his tone hardening, 'who are you to accuse me of dishonesty?'

'Just get out of here and leave me alone!' groaned Lindy against the pillows. 'I want to pack!'

'I'll help you.'

'I don't want your help!'

'No.'

In the silence that ensued after he had uttered that one word she found herself wondering if he had actually risen without her sensing it, and left. Then he spoke again.

'When I spoke of love and Arista I was referring to the exasperated sort of protective affection that can be felt towards someone who's been on the periphery of one's life since childhood. Arista may have looks, but as her personality's so ghastly surely you can understand how few real friends she has?'

Lindy's head rose. 'Why are you telling me this?' she asked, confused and suspicious.

'Because you were so obviously upset when I mentioned my feelings towards her.'

'You're mistaken,' she lied explosively. 'I couldn't give a damn how you feel about her!'

Her face sank back to the pillows, her heart lurching sickeningly. Had she really been that transparent? Of course she had!

'Have it your own way... I've had enough of this!' he exclaimed wearily. 'I suspect this has been a pretty awful day for us both, one way and another.'

'Nobody asked you to go out looking for me!'

'What I was referring to as being awful for me was the thought of your taking off for the mainland in a boat you probably didn't know how to handle—or, even worse, attempting to swim for it——'

'Even I wouldn't be that stupid!' she objected.

'How was I to know that?' he asked, rising. 'It wasn't until I learned of your inordinate fear regarding imprisonment that I was forced to look at things in a different light.' He began walking towards the door. 'I'd hoped that for once we could talk without it deteriorating into a screaming match...there were things I wanted to say.'

'What stopped you just going ahead and saying them?' she flung after him. 'You're not normally the sort of person to hold anything back!'

'No, but then neither am I normally overbearing and violent,' he pointed out wearily. 'And perhaps I'm not prepared to voice what's inside me because I know in my heart of hearts I'd be wasting my breath.' He opened

the door. 'Don't bother ordering any supper for me—
I'm having a bath and going to bed.'

'Niko... are you feeling all right?' The question leapt
involuntarily from her in a small, almost frightened
voice.

'Never felt better, darling,' he drawled. 'And you?'

She sat up on the bed, hugging her knees to her chest
and rocking distractedly back and forth. Why should
she feel guilty? Why should she become racked with
anxiety the instant she imagined she heard a note almost
of despair in his voice? And it *had* been her imagination, she reminded herself bitterly as the drawling
cynicism of his parting shot reverberated in her ears.

He had kept her here against her will; had browbeaten
and bullied her; had terrified her half out of her
wits... and what had she done? Like the complete moron
she undoubtedly was, she had fallen in love with him,
she informed herself savagely. And, what was almost
worse, her insuppressible jealousy of Arista had as good
as told him how she felt.

Driven by the fury of mortification, she hurled herself
from the bed and threw herself into an orgy of packing.
Over an hour later, and the packing done, she took
herself off for yet another bath.

Her mind still churning chaotically, she even contemplated going for a swim, before flinging herself disconsolately into bed.

And it was then that she learned just how uncoop-
erative and punishing love could be. Instead of bolstering
her with memories of all the wrongs he had done her,
she found her mind bombarding her with facts she had
no wish to examine. Such as the fact that, the instant
he had learned of the terrors besetting her, he had released her from them. And the fact that, unlike many

other men, he would never turn his back on a child he had fathered, no matter what the circumstances.

As love took its complete hold on her she was remembering the dizzy, stumbling state he had been in the night before. And she rose from her bed and went to him—love's driving compassion negating her own innate pride.

'Niko?'

His room was in darkness save for the single light at the writing bureau. He was seated at the bureau, his head slumped in his arms.

'Niko!' she gasped, racing, barefoot, to his side.

He turned and half lifted his head.

'Lindy, I . . .' He broke off, kicking aside the chair as he got to his feet and wrapped his arms fiercely around her. 'I've been trying to think straight,' he groaned, burying his face against her hair. 'Everything's been out of perspective for so long—I can't get it right! I *have* to get it right!'

It was the frantic bemusement in his words that brought love aching and unmasked to the surface from within her.

'Niko, you mustn't try so hard,' she whispered, reaching her arms up around him and stroking her fingers lovingly through his hair. 'You've got to give it time—it'll be all right in the end, you know that.'

'Do I?' he muttered, the words so bewildered that a sob of protest choked within her at her own contribution to the state he was in.

'Darling, you've had all the tests and the doctors have told you——'

'You called me darling,' he interrupted hoarsely.

A small ripple of protest shivered through her, then she suddenly relaxed completely—what was the point in pretending?

'Yes—but that's my problem, not yours,' she whispered softly.

'And what's my problem?'

'Impatience,' she sighed. 'Niko, after yesterday, the last thing you needed was all the stress you've had today.'

'Mmm,' he agreed, positioning her more securely in his arms. 'Today was probably the worst day of my life, so far.'

'And that's why you were almost bound to have another attack of...of...'

'Double vision?' he queried helpfully.

Her trouble hadn't been that she was searching for the words, it was simply that she had become acutely distracted by the ways his hands had begun playing almost seductively against her back.

'Yes,' she croaked.

'I'm not experiencing double vision—and haven't all day.'

'Thank heavens for that! Niko...what are you doing?'

'Perhaps I ought to lie down for a while—I'm feeling a little weak,' he stated in a voice that sounded surprisingly strong, given his claim.

And, though he appeared to require her support in reaching the bed, there was nothing to indicate weakness in the hold he maintained on her as she attempted to help him lie down—in fact, there was a noticeable strength in the arms that carried her downwards on to the bed with him.

'Niko, I don't want you to have any worries...especially about my being pregnant, though I really don't feel I am... What I'm trying to say is——'

'Funnily enough, it would make life a lot more straightforward for me if you weren't,' he stated almost conversationally.

'Why funnily?' she exclaimed, slightly thrown by his choice of words. 'Of course it would!'

'You really don't understand, do you, Lindy?' he sighed.

'No—I suppose I don't,' she replied, anxious and troubled by his behaviour and uncertain whether or not to ask him if there were side-effects, other than double vision, that he suffered as a result of his accident.

He shifted his body suddenly, lowering himself till his head rested against her. And, because there was no longer any need in her for pretence, she cradled him to her, trying desperately to block out the terrible realisation that this would be the last time her arms would ever hold him.

'I trained myself,' he murmured cosily, 'till in the end there were few times when I looked at you without being able to find fault with you.'

She closed her eyes, a sick despair filling her as she heard those almost nonsensical words and hoping that her decision to let him have his say, no matter what it might cost her, would do him good rather than harm.

'At times you made it so easy for me...especially when I knew you were lying to me. Such as the night when Russell returned to the hotel to empty the safe.'

'How did you know?' she asked, a feeling almost of relief entering her as she realised that perhaps his words weren't quite as confused as they had first seemed.

'One of the waiters happened to hear your voices and reported to me that Russell had returned.'

'Niko, I honestly didn't know he'd taken all that money that night!'

'Of course you didn't...but can't you understand how easy it was for me to find fault with you?'

'Only too easily,' she sighed, though growing more and more confused. 'But I wanted to tell you the truth that night!'

'And Russell put paid to that by bringing up the threat of prison...I understand all that, Lindy.' As he spoke he moved again—this time reversing their positions until it was she who was cradled against him. 'Lindy, what are you thinking?' he asked softly.

She shook her head, then buried it against him as she fought back the sudden threat of tears.

'Lindy, this is the only way I can think of of doing this...leading you step by step. I don't want you to misjudge me.'

'How can I misjudge you?' she protested disconsolately. 'You're the one who was fed a pack of lies right from the start...how could I possibly expect you to react other than as you did?'

'I can assure you, there was nothing in the least normal about any of my reactions,' he contradicted with a sigh, his fingers playing absent-mindedly against her hair. 'The very first time I saw you you were trying to explain something to one of the maids who spoke very little English. I watched you for a long time and saw you try to mime what you wanted. After a while you collapsed in a giggling heap on the floor...and once you were over your fit of the giggles you looked up at her and you smiled.'

'Did I?' she asked, a catch in her voice as everything in her seemed to slow down almost to a halt.

'Oh, yes—you smiled. And I turned and walked away without ever having made my presence known to you.'

'Why?' whispered Lindy, trying to sit up but finding herself imprisoned against him.

'Because the most ridiculous and illogical thought had flashed through my mind—that I had at last seen a woman I could love . . . and I wanted to escape it.'

'Ridiculous and illogical?' she croaked, barely conscious of uttering the words.

'Most definitely. Especially when that thought kept returning to me. And especially when it turned out she was married. And even more especially when that fact made not the slightest bit of difference to the mindless attraction I felt towards her.'

'And the fact that she gobbled you up with her eyes whenever they looked at you?' she demanded huskily, breaking free to rise and gaze down at him.

'God, how I hated you for that,' he whispered hoarsely, his eyes refusing to meet hers. 'I managed to perform the impossible task of hating you even as I was falling in love with you.'

Her heart seemed to be skipping two in every three beats.

'Niko, why won't you look at me?' she pleaded, a terrible sense of foreboding warning her that his words couldn't be what they had seemed.

'Lindy, just let me do this in my way—step by step. You have to understand that I got no pleasure from learning you weren't married . . . knowing that made me want to hate you all the more.'

She drew away from him, suddenly seeing it all too clearly. She knew nothing of Greek society, except that he belonged to a family that was an esteemed part of it. Being attracted to a married woman was bad enough for him, given his views on such matters, but discovering she was single had obviously struck him as even worse. A Leandros becoming involved with such a social inferior, she thought bitterly—that really would have been the last straw!

'Lindy, can't you understand that I thought you had been his mistress? I was convinced you'd been in league with him and that you still were, despite his having sacrificed you to me with his gambling.'

'It's all right, you don't have to keep going on about it—I understand perfectly,' she told him expressionlessly.

'And you understand why I'd find it so much easier if you weren't pregnant?' he demanded.

'Yes.'

'All right—tell me why.'

She didn't know how she managed to bite back a bitter exclamation at the sheer callousness of that request, but it was fury with herself for having squandered something as precious as love on a man who could make such a request of her that gave her the strength to assemble an answer.

'Most reasonably intelligent people tend to judge others by what they are, not by their social standing, or by what sort of blood happens to run through their veins, as though they were cattle to be bred from.'

He sat up as she finished speaking, his face contorted with rage as he caught hold of her and shook her angrily.

'You're saying you believe that of *me*?' he demanded in outrage. 'My God, I actually thought there was a chance you were falling in love with me!'

'Well, you got it wrong!' she raged, no longer caring what she said. 'Because I love you already! Which only goes to show what a complete imbecile I am! And, believe me, it is possible to love and hate all at the same time, because——'

'Lindy, don't!' he groaned, pulling her against him. 'Why wouldn't you let me take it step by step as I wanted?' he pleaded distractedly, his arms tightening to still her struggles. 'I wanted you to see exactly how it had all seemed from my point of view and perhaps begin to understand why I behaved as I did. I wanted you to understand that it was only because I wanted to kill you when you said you had a choice over whether or not to have our child——'

'Can't *you* understand?' she burst out hysterically. 'I didn't mean it! I couldn't even bring myself to say the word...I wished I'd never even said what I did! Why can't you believe me?'

'I do believe you... Hell, Lindy, that really has nothing to do with what I'm trying to say to you,' he groaned. 'There's only one reason that I'd rather you weren't pregnant—even though there's no other woman on this earth I'd want to bear my children——'

'What did you say?' she croaked, gazing bewilderedly into his face and telling herself that the uncertainty that seemed to mingle with the anger in his expression was merely another shadow created by the poorness of the light.

'Are you ever going to let me finish what I'm trying to say?' he groaned exasperatedly. 'Lindy, I'd like to be able to ask you to marry me in the absolute knowledge that you were aware I was asking you not because there was a chance you were pregnant...but because I love you.'

'Niko, I...you... This isn't fair! Most of the time I've been on this island I've felt I was in danger of losing my mind—now I know I have!'

'That's a relief,' he muttered, giving her an extremely wary look before he suddenly drew her down on to the bed and held her firmly to him. 'That mind of yours was always leaping to disastrously wrong conclusions anyway.'

'Niko...did you just tell me you loved me?' she asked in a dazed, slightly querulous voice.

'Yes, I did. And I really don't understand why you ask in that tone!' he exclaimed indignantly. 'Even Arista spotted it, for heaven's sake! That night she and I were dancing in here...the way I reacted when you got up and left seemed to tell her exactly how I felt about you—and my denials, when she put it to me, didn't sound convincing, even to my own ears.' His arms tightened almost suffocatingly around her. 'So the answer is yes—I did just tell you that I love you...and I do. Darling,' he groaned, burying his face against her hair, 'you can't imagine what a relief it is simply to be able to say those words. And, as for losing one's mind—I'm still not sure where mine is...my only certainty is that I love you.'

She wrapped her arms around his neck, clinging fiercely as more happiness than she could possibly cope with buffeted her unmercifully.

'Oh, Niko, I love you, I love you...Oh, heck, I think I'm going to cry!'

'Don't you dare,' he protested unsteadily. 'The last time you did that it did the most terrible things to areas inside me I never knew existed.'

'I know it did,' she choked, making a concerted effort to gain control of herself. 'And I think that was when I first began to realise I loved you...and I was terrified! And no wonder I was incapable of facing my weird fear of being in prison—I was too preoccupied by the horror of being in love with you!'

'I can't even object to your choice of words,' he muttered with a sigh, 'given that I regarded loving you as equally horrifying.'

'But I also had the horror of discovering jealousy,' she complained from within her cocoon of bliss, butting her head against his in protest as he gave a contented chuckle.

'And I'll go on making you jealous until I get exactly what I want . . . and then you know the rest.'

'What exactly is it you want, and what do you mean—I know the rest?' she exclaimed, her arms tightening exuberantly around his neck.

'Lindy, you're breaking my neck!' he protested, chuckling.

'Niko, I'm so sorry!' she replied, disentwining her arms from around him and stroking him anxiously on the face.

'And so you should be,' he murmured, grinning contentedly up at her as his hands began exploring purposefully against her body. 'We mustn't forget I'm still a convalescent.'

'Of course I wouldn't forget that,' she protested, trying with scant success to ignore the inflammatory progress of his hands as she peered anxiously down at him. 'Niko, you're not seeing two of me, are you?'

He shook his head. 'But I'm going to need round-the-clock attention to ensure I follow my doctors' orders. In fact, the sort of undivided attention that starts off with a honeymoon and extends over a lifetime would do the trick . . . which brings me back to *exactly* what I want.' He gave a soft chuckle as she discreetly dragged the back of her hand across her cheeks. 'I hope that threatened fit of the weeps isn't about to materialise.'

She shook her head vigorously. 'I think I must be the happiest person in the world,' she choked.

'I hate to argue, now that we're such good friends,' he teased, cupping her face in his hands and almost blinding her with the love blazing from his eyes, 'but I've a feeling that I'm the happiest person in the world—and I'd be absolutely certain I was were you to tell me you'll marry me.'

She screwed her eyes tightly shut and then nodded.

'Was that a yes?' he chuckled.

She nodded again.

'I take it that was a yes that it was a yes,' he murmured in tones of long-suffering patience.

With a soft squeal of indignation she slipped from his hands and flung herself against him.

'You don't know how close you came to being drowned in a deluge of tears of pure joy!' she exclaimed softly. 'And yes, yes, yes, I'll marry you!'

'Thank God for that!' he intoned piously, the expression in his eyes a mixture of wicked teasing and darkening need as he lifted her body fully on to his.

'Niko—what's the rest, that you said I know all about?' she murmured distractedly, her senses leaping riotously as his hands returned to their inciting exploration of her body.

'Oh, that,' he whispered distractedly against her parted mouth as her body began to tremble in seductive impatience against his.

'Yes, that!' She shivered as his lips brushed maddeningly against hers and his touch sent electrifying shocks sizzling through her body.

'I think it was that you'd never have reason to be jealous again—and you won't,' he replied with a sharp gasp as her hands took their lead from his. 'I told you how I felt about marriage and that love would be the only mistress I'd ever have... as you're my love, I think you should be able to work out the rest for yourself,' he murmured unsteadily.

'I just have, and it's beautiful,' she choked.

With a softly groaned laugh he turned their entwined bodies. 'Love me,' he whispered, just as he had once before, but this time with the open commitment of love ringing in his voice.

'Forever.'

Next Month's Romances

Each month you can choose from a world of variety in romance with Mills & Boon. Below are the new titles to look out for next month, why not ask either Mills & Boon Reader Service or your Newsagent to reserve you a copy of the titles you want to buy — just tick the titles you would like to order and either post to Reader Service or take it to any Newsagent and ask them to order your books.

Please save me the following titles:	Please tick	✓
PAST LOVING	Penny Jordan	
WINTER OF DREAMS	Susan Napier	
KNIGHT TO THE RESCUE	Miranda Lee	
OUT OF NOWHERE	Patricia Wilson	
SECOND CHANCE FOR LOVE	Susanne McCarthy	
MORE THAN A DREAM	Emma Richmond	
REVENGE	Natalie Fox	
YESTERDAY AND FOREVER	Sandra Marton	
NO GENTLEMAN	Kate Walker	
CATALINA'S LOVER	Vanessa Grant	
OLD LOVE, NEW LOVE	Jennifer Taylor	
A FRENCH ENCOUNTER	Cathy Williams	
THE TRESPASSER	Jane Donnelly	
A TEMPTING SHORE	Dana James	
A LOVE TO LAST	Samantha Day	
A PLACE OF WILD HONEY	Ann Charlton	

If you would like to order these books from Mills & Boon Reader Service please send £1.70 per title to: Mills & Boon Reader Service, P.O. Box 236, Croydon, Surrey, CR9 3RU and quote your Subscriber No:...(If applicable) and complete the name and address details below. Alternatively, these books are available from many local Newsagents including W.H.Smith, J.Menzies, Martins and other paperback stockists from 14th August 1992.

Name:...

Address:...

....Post Code:......................

To Retailer: If you would like to stock M&B books please contact your regular book/magazine wholesaler for details.

You may be mailed with offers from other reputable companies as a result of this application. If you would rather not take advantage of these opportunities please tick box ☐